# Looking *for* Cardenio

# Looking *for* Cardenio

Jean Rae Baxter

Seraphim Editions

The publisher gratefully acknowledges the financial assistance of the Canada Council for the Arts and the Ontario Arts Council.

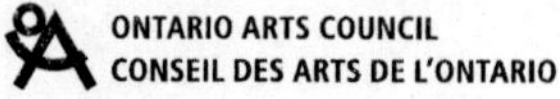


**Library and Archives Canada Cataloguing in Publication**

Baxter, Jean Rae
Looking for Cardenio / Jean Rae Baxter.

ISBN 978-0-9808879-0-7

1. Shakespeare, William, 1564-1616–Authorship–Fiction.
I. Title.

PS8603.A935L66 2008 C813'.6 C2008-901903-2

Editor: Kerry J. Schooley
Cover Photo: Janice Jackson
Author Photo: Today's Faces Photography
Cover Design and Typography: Julie McNeill, McNeill Design Arts

Published in 2008 by
Seraphim Editions
238 Emerald St. N.
Hamilton, ON
Canada L8L 5K8

Printed and bound in Canada

In memory of my husband
John Scott Baxter

*This thou perceivest, which makes thy love more strong,*
*To love that well which thou must leave ere long.*

# One

I was forty when I met Sebastian. It happened in June, at the Learned Societies Conference in Toronto, where I had been invited to lecture on imagery in *The Tempest.* In honour of the occasion I had invested in a Holt Renfrew suit, splurging because I wanted to look terrific when I stepped onto the lecture platform.

Sebastian had not actually attended my lecture, he later admitted – simply drifted into the reception that followed. The initial attraction had been canapés on a long table and waiters proffering glasses of wine.

I was struck by his youth and by the easy grace with which he strolled about the room, an expression of aloof amusement on his face. He wore a short-sleeve, open-neck shirt, like most of the men present. Only academics scheduled to deliver a paper wore suits. A few older scholars had donned their professorial gowns.

Sebastian gravitated to the group of people standing around offering me congratulations. When the others had moved off, Sebastian remained. He was blond. Grey eyes fringed with long lashes. Perhaps he was not so young as I had initially thought, for he had one of those fine-boned English faces that look boyish into the thirties.

He was, he said, newly arrived in Toronto, and at first glance he had determined that the city wasn't as provincial as expected.

His condescension nettled me. "Is this your first visit to the Colonies?" I asked.

The flicker of his eyes showed that he caught the sarcasm.

"First time in Canada." He plucked a glass of white wine from a passing tray. "Would you like to show me around town?"

By answering "Not particularly," I could have put a stop to things before they began. I was not sure that I wanted to know him better. But I had no plans for the evening, and I was in the mood to celebrate. My paper on *The Tempest* had been received with solid applause, and I knew that word of my success would soon reach my colleagues at Melrose University, confirming that Dr. Deirdre Gunn was a rising star in the academic firmament.

Why spend the evening watching a movie alone in my hotel room? I was already dressed for dinner at the best restaurant in town, for I had blown my clothes budget for the year to buy that suit – sage-green silk, which emphasized the colour of my eyes and brought out the warm tints of my auburn hair. Here was an opportunity to gain a bonus dividend from my investment.

I gave my new acquaintance a cool smile. "Have you been to the top of the CN Tower? It may sound crass, but the view from the revolving restaurant is spectacular."

"That might be interesting." He paused. "If I can book a table, will you join me this evening for dinner?" Another pause. "My name is Sebastian Pomeroy."

Pomeroy. The King's Apple. A name with a thousand years of history. His forebears had come from Normandy with William the Conqueror. And he looked like a Sebastian – not the martyred one pierced with arrows, but a quintessentially English Sebastian. He had the accent to go with it, like Tony Blair's but with a husky tone I found enticing. The fact that he was young did not disturb me: I've had friends of all ages.

"It's Friday," I said, deliberately non-committal. "A reservation might be difficult."

"I'm staying at the Park Plaza." He smiled. "If you'd walk over with me, I could ring from my room."

"Yes," I said, "I suppose you could."

If he could afford the Park Plaza, he could afford the revolving restaurant.

"What brought you here?" I asked as we strolled up Philosophers Walk to Bloor Street.

"Oxford didn't agree with me." He shrugged. "Or perhaps it was the other way around. After I was sent down, the family thought I might read for my degree in some other country."

"In what subject?"

"Probably English literature. I'm useless at subjects where one has to learn facts. With literature, one makes it up as one goes along."

"Up to a point."

"Would you care to come up while I telephone?" he asked as we entered the hotel.

"I'll wait in the lobby."

I eased myself into a sumptuous black leather armchair. When he returned, he had a satisfied air. Our reservation was for six o'clock. While in his room, he had changed to a light jacket with Savile Row tailoring, the perfect complement to my suit.

I felt a certain lightness of heart as we started out together. Sebastian looked relaxed and pleased as he gazed out the taxi window. It occurred to me that he was, like me, accustomed to admiration from the opposite sex.

We dined on lobster parfait, bouillabaisse and roast crown of lamb while the restaurant slowly turned, presenting views of the city and the countryside, of Lake Ontario and the Island Airport and a distant shadow that might have been the Niagara Escarpment.

Sebastian, clearly to the manner born, knew how to choose the right wines, how to order, how to address the waiter. He was courteous and poised. From the way his eyes wandered over my silk-clad bosom, I recognized at least some of what he found attractive about me. Yet there was no flirtation while we discussed the settlement of Upper Canada, and drifted from there to the glaciers that had gouged out the Great Lakes. Nor was there any mention of sex, apart from one exchange as we left the CN Tower and glanced up at its priapic eminence jutting into the night sky.

"Phallic," he said.

"The world's tallest free-standing erection," I agreed.

"Quite."

He raised his arm to hail a passing taxi. It stopped for us. "The Park Plaza," he said, without consulting me.

In the cab, he put his arm around my shoulders and leaned towards me. My hands went up, obeying the instinct to push him away. But when he kissed me, the warmth of his mouth and the scent of his aftershave undermined my intentions. My still unspoken protest vanished like mist as my hands sank onto his shoulders. I returned his kiss, and then gently pulled away.

"Not here." I took a deep breath.

Sebastian smiled as if he knew exactly what I meant. While the taxi crawled north on Bay Street through the Friday night crowd, I watched the play of moving lights upon his pale skin. The word lumière entered my mind. The hum of traffic through the window glass was like a caress. Son et lumière. Hypnotized by sound and light. I didn't think about how it would end. I imagined nothing more definite than our two bodies naked in a bed.

Morning woke me with a shaft of sunlight slanting between the drapes. On the floor was the tangle of our clothes, of our mingled underwear. I glanced at the clock. 10:00 a.m.

Jumping out of bed, I dashed into the bathroom to shower. The checkout time at my hotel was eleven. At four hundred dollars per night, I couldn't afford to be late.

Back in the bedroom, I scrambled into my clothes. Sebastian protested, "Surely you're not leaving?"

"I have to get back to my hotel."

"So soon?"

"Unfortunately, yes. I must pack. I have a train to catch." I wasn't going to tell him about the four hundred dollars.

I would have bestowed a parting kiss, but instinct warned that if I approached too close he would pull me back into bed. I flew from the room.

"Taxi?" the doorman asked.

"No thanks." The subway entrance was close by.

At one o'clock my train pulled out of Union Station. I leaned back in my seat, relaxed and ready to enjoy the blissful state of suspended animation that is one of the great delights of railway travel.

What would Dr. Lola Buckmaster think if she could see me now? When I was in grad school at King's College almost twenty years ago, the formidable Dr. Buckmaster, doyenne of Women's Studies, had counselled me. "Pretty women aren't taken seriously," she had warned. I had ignored her advice. In my opinion, the world would have taken Dr. Buckmaster every bit as seriously if she had not burned her brassieres. Looking good in a sweater has no harmful effect on the brain. What idiot created the notion that a fully packed bra is the sign of an empty mind?

I had published my first book, *Textual Problems in Shakespeare's Late Plays,* at the age of twenty-nine, and with that publication began to build my reputation for sound scholarship. Now my years of hard work were about to pay off.

In the fourteen years since I received my doctorate (Magna cum Laude) I had been at seven different universities, spending the past two years as an assistant professor at Melrose. But things were about to change. Tenure, which had long eluded me, was finally within my grasp. I stood at the threshold of full acceptance in the academic world. After one more year, if all went well, I would become a permanent faculty member.

In three hours the Toronto/Montreal train would stop at Atherton, the home of Melrose University. Dozens of e-mails would be waiting for me. But until then, as the clickety-clack of the train wheels assured me, I could do nothing about them at all.

Relaxed, almost euphoric, I gazed out the window while the train rolled by the green hills of Northumberland County, travelling through villages and towns, then further east, passing miles of scruffy swamps and limestone farms.

On the approach to Atherton, the railway tracks ran parallel to the road, both road and tracks arcing around a pretty bay where sailboats scudded across blue water. A small church stood on the shore. As the train slowed, I caught a glimpse of a wedding party posing for pictures on the church steps. It was a big wedding. Six bridesmaids in dresses of primrose yellow flanked the happy couple. The bride, gowned in white, held a pink bouquet. The groom wore a tuxedo and carried a baby in his arms. Their baby? I supposed it must be.

Twenty years ago, you never would have seen a sight like that.

# Two

Through July and August, course preparation fully occupied my time and thoughts. In the fall, I would be introducing a post-graduate course in textual criticism. That, along with my undergraduate Shakespeare course, usually taken by students in second year, and my section of English 101, would make up a full program.

My Toronto fling seldom, if ever, entered my thoughts. September arrived. On the first day of term, as I entered the crowded hall to give my Introduction to Shakespeare lecture, the face of Sebastian Pomeroy was the last thing I expected to see.

But there he was, sitting in the front row. I tried to ignore him. But whenever I looked up, I saw his gaze fixed on me. Whenever I looked down, I could not find my place in my lecture notes.

"Shakespeare wrote six plays," I informed the class. The students exchanged startled glances. I corrected myself. "That is to say, we shall study six plays that Shakespeare wrote."

The students tittered.

If I hadn't known the material by rote, I don't know how I would have gotten through the hour. When the lecture ended, Sebastian was waiting at the door.

"What are you doing here?" I asked.

"The University of Toronto didn't accept me. But I don't mind. It should be easier to get a degree here at Melrose, with you to help me."

"Don't count on that."

"I meant in little ways."

"Not even in very little ways. You must transfer out of this course. I don't want you in my class."

"I fail to see why."

"Think about it." I folded my arms across my chest, my sheaf of lecture notes clutched as a shield. "How could you and I have a normal professor-student relationship?"

"I didn't anticipate that we would."

"No." I stepped back. "There's no way you can stay in this class."

His eyebrows rose. "What do you suggest?"

"You could drop English."

"It's my best subject."

"Then transfer to some other course."

He sulked but, seeing the point, switched to the survey course, English 201.

I kept him out of my class but, foolishly, not out of my bed.

Melrose is a small university. An affair with a student was not a prudent move. I knew the risks.

So why did I do it? Because Sebastian's body was beautiful? Because he was terrific in bed? Because this was easy sex with no possibility of commitment? Sometimes there's no simple answer to a question like that. Ask Bill Clinton. I did it because I could.

Sebastian's apartment was on the other side of town. I never went there. For him to visit me was more discreet. My neighbours, if they noticed his visits, would assume that he came for tutoring.

He had enrolled in Ancient History, Urban Geography, Philosophy, Sociology and English 201. As the weeks went by, he never mentioned what he was learning in any of his courses. Although curious, I did not ask. To question him about his studies would have underlined the awkwardness of our relationship – awkwardness that only I seemed to feel. But from a few discreet inquiries, I learned that Sebastian seldom attended lectures or handed in assignments. I had suspected from the start that this scion of the English aristocracy was unsuited to hard work. His brain was not the most active part of his anatomy.

It was one week before the start of final examinations, after an afternoon of delicious dalliance, that things started to go wrong. I was stroking Sebastian's smooth thighs when he said, without warning: "Deirdre, I'd appreciate it awfully if you could find out what questions will be on my English exam."

My hand stopped moving. "How can you suggest such a thing?"

"I'm not asking for the answers. Just the questions."

"No."

"If I fail, I'll lose half of my allowance."

I sat up. "In that case, you should go back to England."

"If I set foot in England, I'll lose my entire allowance."

"Was your family that desperate to get rid of you?" Suddenly I was aware that I might be desperate to get rid of him too.

"There was quite a stink at Oxford," he said ruefully.

"Over a girl?"

"Woman, actually. A Master's wife. Father was not amused."

"So that's why you came to Canada."

"Not directly. New Zealand first, for a couple of years. A spot of trouble there too, I'm afraid."

"Another woman?"

"Regrettably."

"Sebastian, how old are you?" He looked shocked at the question. Age was not something we discussed.

"Twenty-two."

"How long have you been carrying on like this?"

He paused. "Since I was thirteen. There was a very pretty upstairs maid . . ." A trace of a smile. "Servants have always been kind to me."

Servants! I felt a sudden chill. If servants weren't kind to Young Master, they could start looking for work elsewhere. Was that my status in Sebastian's eyes?

I soon found out. When I continued to refuse to supply him with the examination questions, he went to the Dean of Studies with a complaint about me.

It was during the final week of May that the Dean of Studies' secretary summoned me. Not a good sign. If there had been something pleasant to communicate, Dr. Ian McBroom would have phoned me himself. As I entered his outer office, I had a premonition, which the secretary did nothing to dispel.

With a curt nod in my direction, she spoke to the intercom. “Dr. Gunn is here.”

“You may send her in.”

His secretary opened the door. Across half an acre of hardwood floor, Dr. McBroom regarded me from behind his vast mahogany desk. The oversize leather chair in which he sat must have been inherited from a larger predecessor, for the Dean of Studies was a wisp of a man, perhaps five-foot-four, at most one hundred and thirty pounds. The chair would have held two men his size.

The large oil portrait on the wall behind Dr. McBroom further diminished him. Bearded, dark and heavy browed, Melrose University's first Principal, Douglas Mackenzie, D.D., regarded me sternly from a massive gilded frame.

The mahogany desk and the two straight-backed chairs that faced it sat on a thick, blue carpet. As I approached, high heels clicking on the hardwood floor, I tripped over the carpet's edge. My arms flailed, giving flight to my final trace of self-assurance.

“Please take a seat.”

My cheeks burning, I sat down.

Dr. McBroom's head reared back, and he looked down his long nose at me.

“Dr. Gunn, you realize that a small university like Melrose depends heavily upon endowments.”

“Of course.”

“We began as a Presbyterian institution, and our patrons still cherish our founders' values: hard work and strict morality." He picked up his black fountain pen and rolled it between his fingers.

I couldn't help raising my eyes to the portrait of Douglas Mackenzie, D.D. His eyes reproached me. *Moral turpitude,* they seemed to say.

"The granting of tenure is at the discretion of the University Senate. In your case, Dr. Gunn, the decision was difficult, for your publications, your teaching and your scholarship are exemplary." He cleared his throat. "But there are other, less pleasant considerations. Unfortunately, we received a report, fully substantiated, of impropriety involving a student. The University Senate dealt with the case in camera. Since the student was not in one of your classes, this was not, strictly speaking, a case of abuse of authority. But it was certainly a matter of poor judgment. And therefore, with regret, the Senate determined that it would not be in Melrose University's best interests to make you an offer of tenure."

Fired. I walked like a robot to my car. Once inside, I leaned against the back of the seat, clenched my teeth and closed my eyes, feeling the frustration that had dogged my entire career. "Christ, it was only sex," I muttered. Dr. McBroom made it sound as if I had seduced Sebastian in Toronto and lured him here to continue my enjoyment of sexual favours.

Now what was I going to do?

# Three

It was 10:00 p.m. and I was in the Arts Building clearing out my office on the fourth floor – the office that used to be mine. The books that I wanted to keep were already in cartons for UPS to pick up in the morning. Except for one last load, those I didn't want were spread out on a table in the English Department lounge under a sign I had written in black marker: "If you want these books, they're yours. Deirdre."

While I was pushing the janitor's dolly from the lounge back to my office for the final load, I heard the elevator stop. I could not see who got out, because the elevator was down the hall and around a corner. But I could hear footsteps echo in the empty corridor, coming toward me. I walked faster.

The tread sounded like a man's. Probably one of my colleagues had stopped by to pick up something from his office. I didn't suppose that he had come to see me, but if he did see me, he might wish to chat or to express his sympathy, and I wanted none of that. Shoving the dolly inside my office, I quickly shut the door.

I took a few deep breaths. Now what? Maybe I should do some work while I waited for him to leave. There's always work, even for unemployed academics. I could try to finish my review of the latest idiotic book claiming to prove that Shakespeare didn't write Shakespeare's plays. Glad that I had not yet cleaned out my desk, I sat down and slid open the drawer that held my notes. But as soon as I looked over my scribbles, I gave up. I was too depressed for mental effort.

Lifting my eyes from the page, I stared at the empty nail on the opposite wall where my PhD diploma had hung for the past two years. This time, I had hoped it would be permanent. But it hadn't worked out. I was forty-one years old, and back to looking for a teaching position in a saturated market.

The footsteps were closer. They stopped, started again, stopped, and started. It sounded as if someone was pausing at every office door to read its nameplate. Then it wasn't a colleague.

I stiffened, wished that I had locked the door. Maybe under some circumstances the pen is mightier than the sword, but as a defensive weapon a ballpoint is useless. The footsteps stopped. There was a knock.

I meant to ignore it. But the door opened.

At the threshold stood a short, stout man, tweedy in a shopworn way, with a navy-cut beard like King George V in old photographs. His hair was brown, greying at the temples. He made no move to enter but waited at the threshold, holding a zippered binder.

"Well, Deirdre, I haven't seen you for a long time."

"You are ... ?"

He did not answer, but stood his ground and took my inspection patiently. He looked familiar, but the penny didn't drop until I tried to picture his face without the beard, and then I caught my breath. George Pinkus, my old classmate.

"G-g-g-george!" I stammered. "What are you doing here? How did you get in?"

"By tipping the caretaker."

He entered – not waiting to be asked – stepped around the cartons of books and pulled up a chair.

"What's this all about?" I said.

"I wanted to see you." He looked around, his eyes scanning the empty floor-to-ceiling bookcases.

"Me? Why?"

For twenty years he'd had no more need to see me than I'd had to see him. We were never friends. Although we had started out as classmates, George was expelled for plagiarism in his final year. Thinking nobody would notice, he had cribbed his major essay from a PhD dissertation that he had dug up in the university library. Professors are smarter than the average student realizes, and George Pinkus was less than average. Pathetic? Probably. But even then I'd had little sympathy.

For years I had not given him a thought. Yet here he was sitting in my office, looking at me with an expression that was more smirk than smile.

"So what have you been doing with yourself?" I didn't know what else to say.

"Tutoring. Writing essays for students who'll pay."

"You what?" I started at this frank admission.

"You heard me," he said.

"That's a criminal offence."

"Writing them isn't. Just using them." He gave a short laugh. "Don't knock it. From what I hear, you may end up joining me."

"George ..." I felt my blood rushing to my face. "I don't know why you're here. But you'd better leave."

"I know your situation. Maybe I don't teach at a university. But I have contacts. I hear the gossip." He leaned forward. "Screwing a student! At your age! You'll never get another position at any decent university."

I stood up, pointed to the door. "I'll call security."

He didn't budge. "It's called harassment," he said.

"He was a consenting adult, twenty-two years old."

"Naughty, naughty."

"Get out!"

"Not so fast. You need to hear what I have to say."

I didn't know why George wanted to talk to me, but it surely couldn't be about my morals. I stood facing him, both hands planted on my desk, trying to stare him down.

"Get to the point."

"Very well." He harrumphed and puffed out his chest. "I have a way to make you famous, respectable and rich. With my help, you can thumb your nose at Melrose and pick your next appointment to any university in the English-speaking world."

"Do tell."

"No need for sarcasm. Have you ever heard of a play called *Cardenio?*"

"Yes."

"Have you read it?"

"You know perfectly well that I couldn't have read it."

"What do you know about it?"

"As much as anyone in Shakespeare studies. It's reputed to be by Shakespeare. Probably John Fletcher had a hand in it. It was acted twice at court and probably had a few public performances at the Globe Theatre. Then it was lost."

"Lost and found," he said. "There's a manuscript copy, and I have it."

It isn't often that I'm speechless. Of course I didn't believe him. There was one chance in a million that such a manuscript could survive undiscovered for nearly four hundred years. Even if it did exist, how would someone like George Pinkus get his hands on it?

"You don't believe me," he laughed. "You're gulping like a fish."

"Of course I don't believe you. Where would you have gotten such a thing?"

"Remember the stacks in the old King's College Library, way down in the basement?"

"Yes." As a student, I'd spent hours there, poring through ancient folios and quartos piled haphazardly on the shelves, even on the floor. Moldy leather covers. Worm tunnels through the pages. No climate controls. Senior students had access to the stacks. No security. No buzzers to sound an alarm if somebody snuck out a book. So far as I had known at the time, nobody did. But that had been a different, more honourable world.

"You found it there?" I said.

"Draw your own conclusions."

"But there weren't any manuscripts in the stacks. Not one." I paused. The fact that I had seen none didn't prove there hadn't been any. God knows what had been in the stacks before King's College built its new library, with climate controls and special security for those rare old volumes.

My eyes went straight to George's zippered binder. Feeling like an atheist who has just received a visit from the angel Gabriel, I said: "You have it here?"

His stubby fingers patted the binder. "I thought this would be right up your alley."

"Then you know my field?"

"I've followed your career. There's little you've published that I haven't read."

"Really? Why would you go to the trouble?"

"No need to be sarcastic. I photocopied the first page. If you have a serious interest, I'll show it to you."

A serious interest in Shakespeare's lost play? Was he kidding?

"Yes," I said calmly. "I do have a serious interest."

He unzipped the binder and placed a single photocopied sheet on the desk.

"ACT THE FIRST. SCENE I" The heading stated. The name Cardenio introduced the opening speech. So far as I could tell from one photocopied page, the manuscript was in reasonably good condition – no wormholes or tears. But the handwriting! Was it possible?

George said, "You look like you're about to faint."

"Secretary ...." For a minute I was incapable of even fumbling speech.

"What's that about a secretary?"

I pulled thoughts and words together. "Two forms of handwriting were in common use in Shakespeare's time: the older secretary hand, which is difficult for us to read today, and the newer Italian hand then coming into fashion. The Italian, which was more like modern handwriting, eventually took over. But this is written in the secretary hand."

"So?"

"There are six authentic Shakespeare signatures in existence. All are in the secretary hand."

Now it was George's mouth that hung open. "You mean … ?"

"I mean nothing. Merely speculation."

"Could this be Shakespeare's own handwriting? Is that what you're thinking?"

"Don't get your hopes up. Thousands of people besides Shakespeare used the secretary hand. It's a small argument in support, but I can't tell much from one photocopied page. I need to see the actual manuscript. The whole thing."

"Be reasonable." George gave an unsteady smile. "You don't see the manuscript until we've come to terms."

"Terms? What are you proposing?"

"It's simple. I have no reputation for scholarship. I don't even have a BA degree. That's why I've come to you. For years I've followed your career. It must be someone like you who announces the discovery of the manuscript."

"Like me!" Though my thoughts were swirling, I understood the implications of everything he said.

"Exactly. You bring out the first edition. You write the books. You go on the lecture circuit. Oprah Winfrey interviews you – "

"Enough! I get the picture. *Cardenio* makes me rich and famous. What do you get out of it?"

"Fifty per cent."

"Of what?"

"Of everything, plus the right to approve any sale of the actual manuscript, in case you feel philanthropic and want to donate it for a tax credit to our *alma mater.*"

"Not your *alma mater,*" I said. "As you just reminded me, you didn't graduate."

George flinched.

He cleared his throat. "Fifty percent of royalties from any book you write about *Cardenio.* Fifty percent of the profit from lectures and interviews. Fifty per cent of your salary above a base amount calculated on the average salary of English professors at Canadian universities – ninety thousand a year at current levels."

His proposal left me staggered. "Fifty per cent is high."

"It is. And the deal will last a lifetime. So what do you say?"

I thought fast. Any manuscript of *Cardenio* would be worth millions. An autograph copy – one in Shakespeare's handwriting – would be priceless. The rewards, in terms of money and scholarly fame, were inestimable.

"I'll think it over," I said. "First, I need to assure myself that the manuscript is authentic."

"Of course."

"When can I see it?"

"I'll bring it here tomorrow night."

"No good. I turn in my keys first thing in the morning. Better come to my house."

"Where do you live?"

"I thought you'd know that, along with everything else."

I told him the address, suggested nine o'clock.

After George left, I sat at my desk for half an hour. I told myself to be sensible. A man who earns his living by helping students to cheat is not a man who values scholarly integrity. The manuscript must be a hoax. On the other hand, to forge a whole play would involve so much: the age and type of paper, the ink, the pen, and the penmanship. George couldn't do it. Could anyone?

There was another problem: if I did agree to George's proposal, I would have to produce a provenance for the manuscript. The simplest way to start would be to search the archives at King's College for a record of purchase, gift or legacy. But how could I ask the assistance of King's College in tracking down the history of a manuscript that was not in its possession? Every sort of awkward question would arise.

If I knew how and when King's College had acquired the manuscript, I might be able to follow the links back through time. But the first link in the chain was missing, leaving me not knowing how to begin.

*I'm getting ahead of myself,* I thought as I loaded the dolly with books for the last time. The manuscript might be a forgery. But if it were a forgery, would George bring it to *me* for validation? Not if he knew it was a fake: Unless he thought I could be bought.

# Four

Once home, I checked for e-mails. A couple of dozen waited in my Inbox. There were the usual investment opportunities and offers to increase the size of my penis, several invitations to art gallery openings and book launches, and three messages from Sebastian. I could hear his petulant voice as I read:

> Deirdre, I was terribly hurt when you wouldn't find out for me what was going to be on the exam. It's not as though I wanted the answers. Anyway, I'm sorry about the way it turned out. I didn't mean to get you sacked. Love, Sebastian.

He was sorry! "Not as sorry as I am," I growled at the screen and punched "Delete." Why had he gone to the Dean if he didn't want to destroy my career? Was the boy incapable of foresight? Twenty-two is old enough to have some sense.

I clicked his second message:

> Deirdre. I don't know how many times you expect me to apologize. You act like you don't want to see me again, and I don't see how that's possible. I'm waiting for you to say that I'm forgiven. Love, Sebastian.

I sighed. Truly, I would miss Sebastian. But his treachery

was beyond forgiveness. As soon as I had read his third and last e-mail, I would delete him from my life:

> Deirdre. You haven't left me a message all day, and I've been checking every ten minutes. How can you treat me like this? I'll do anything for you, absolutely anything, if you'll give me another chance. Love, Sebastian

I snorted. What could Sebastian do for me? Nothing. Let him grovel! But George Pinkus had something to offer. And I did not mean sex. Love entanglements had already caused me too many problems. If I had taken as much care about my personal life as I did about scholarship, I would be a tenured professor by now, enjoying respect and security. But no. I had jumped too eagerly into too many beds. "If you make your bed, you must lie in it," my father used to say, speaking more literally than he knew.

What now? Before seeing the manuscript, I needed to review what was known about *Cardenio*. Too bad my books were all packed in cartons, sitting in my former office. But probably the Internet could tell me something beyond the facts I already knew. I glanced at my watch. Twelve-thirty. It shouldn't take long to Google *Cardenio*. How many entries could there be for a play that vanished nearly four hundred years ago?

The answer was a shock. Forty-nine thousand, four hundred entries! Not bad for a lost play. Out of curiosity, I Googled *Hamlet* to get a comparison. Thirteen million. Mind-boggled, I decided that my search could wait until morning. My muscles were tired from shoving books around. It was time for a hot soak in the tub and a good night's sleep.

But my mind wouldn't quit. Over and over, it replayed the scene with George. Had it been a mistake to suggest that the manuscript might be an autograph copy? I should have played that down. Yet it could be.

Shakespeare's draft of the play, which was called the "foul copy," would obviously be in his own handwriting. When satisfied that no further polishing was needed, he would either prepare his own "fair copy" to deliver to the theatre, or take the draft to a professional scrivener for recopying. Which was more likely? That would depend on how busy he was with other projects.

The fair copy delivered to the theatre would have served as the prompt copy, "the book," from which the "book-keeper" transcribed the actors' parts, the speeches they had to learn. No actor received a copy of the entire play. Until a play was published, there might have been only that one single copy of the complete text.

The fact that the manuscript was in the secretary hand meant that it *could* be an autograph copy, not that it must be. A professional scrivener might have used the secretary hand. It was falling out of favour, but not obsolete. With only six authenticated Shakespeare signatures as a basis for comparison, even a handwriting expert would hesitate to make a final determination.

As soon as a play had been printed for public sale, the practice was to destroy all manuscript copies – one reason why Elizabeth and Jacobean play manuscripts are so rare. But *Cardenio* never was published. Why not? The simplest explanation is that no copy survived when the Globe Theatre burned to the ground in June 1613, mere months after the play's first performance.

Shakespeare retired and returned to Stratford. John Fletcher, who may have collaborated with him in writing *Cardenio,* was busy with other plays, making his mark as Shakespeare's successor. Probably neither man had the enthusiasm or the time to reconstruct what had been lost.

For whatever reason, when Shakespeare's colleagues assembled his plays for publication in the *First Folio* in 1623, *Cardenio* was not among them.

I tossed in my bed, summing up the possibilities. The manuscript in George's possession might be an autograph copy. It might be a copy transcribed by a scrivener from the playwright's final draft. It might be a cobbled-together version assembled from actors' individual parts, full of errors and omissions, and embellished with bits of each actor's own invention. Or it might be a fraud.

The phone rang. Half asleep, I reached for it.

"Good morning, Dr. Gunn. Sorry to disturb you." It was Iris McPherson, the English Department's semi-competent office administrator. "We need your keys. I had to use my own to let UPS into ... uh ... your office."

I looked at the clock. Nearly ten-thirty. The day had begun without my knowing it. My books were already on their way across the city.

"I can't bring the keys now. I have to be home for UPS."

"Well, Professor Burton is here ..."

My successor. He didn't lose much time. His teaching duties would not begin until September, yet here he was in mid-June, setting up camp.

"I'll bring them as soon as I can." I paused, suddenly unable to face setting foot in the Arts Building or dealing with Mrs. McPherson in her shapeless cardigan and baggy skirt. "No. I have a better idea. I'll send the keys by taxi."

"Is that a reliable way to deliver them?"

"Mrs. McPherson, if they don't arrive within one hour, you can sue me."

I dragged myself downstairs and made coffee. After a jolt of caffeine, I felt better. I dressed quickly, pulling on sweatpants and an old shirt – my work-at-home uniform. Soon UPS would arrive with nineteen cartons of books, and I had nowhere to shelve them. Every bookcase in the house was full, though the books in them were not mine.

Nor was the house. Its owner was Archibald Weaver, presently residing in the State of California. Professor Weaver, author of *The Influence of Plato on Contemporary Thought,* was capping his illustrious career with a five-year appointment at UCLA. In three years he would return to reclaim his home.

I was the house-sitter, responsible for looking after it until his return. Not a bad arrangement. I paid utilities. He paid the rest. A black cat named Socrates came with the house. Socrates and I were friends.

I carried a second mug of coffee into the living room. It was a comfortable space. Slightly scuffed brown leather chairs and sofa. A Persian carpet. Marble fireplace flanked by floor-to-ceiling shelves loaded with philosophy books.

Professor Weaver had given me permission to pack up his books to make room for mine. Until now, I had not needed to do so because my office – my former office – had three walls of bookshelves, and I had done most of my professional reading there.

Despite an urge to clear the bookshelves before UPS arrived, the scholar in me wanted to look at those forty-nine thousand, four hundred Google entries.

The phone rang. Mrs. McPherson again, asking about the damn keys.

"It's been over an hour," she said pointedly. "Dr. Burton has other things to do."

Oh, hell. I'd completely forgotten. I wanted to tell her to stuff Dr. Burton and the keys, but restrained myself.

"The cab is on its way," I lied. "When I phoned earlier, the taxis were all tied up for some reason. Please give Dr. Burton my apologies."

This time I did call the cab. By the time it pulled up at the curb, I had the keys in a sealed envelope, properly addressed. I gave the driver twenty bucks and sent him on his way.

Now it was noon, and I hadn't eaten yet. I wandered into the kitchen. The yellow eyes of Socrates, sitting on the outside window ledge, accused me through the glass. I let him in, poured kibble into his bowl and bran flakes into mine. After shovelling the bran flakes into my mouth, I left the empty bowl in the sink, went into the study, and got to work.

A few taps on the keyboard brought up what I wanted. I took notes.

1612 John Shelton translates *Don Quixote* into English.

1613 The King's Men perform *Cardenio* at The Globe Theatre.

Payment by Privy Council to John Hemings, in charge of the King's Men, for performing six plays at Court, including *Cardenno* [sic]. *Cardenio* is performed before the Duke of Savoy's ambassador and at the wedding festivities of King James' daughter Elizabeth.

The Globe Theatre burns down.

1614 Rebuilt Globe Theatre opens. No references to Shakespeare, now living in Stratford.

1616 Shakespeare makes his will (March 25) and dies (April 23).

1623 Publication of the *First Folio* of Shakespeare's plays. Thirty-six are included. *Cardenio* not among them.

1642 The Puritans close the theatres.

1644 Globe Theatre demolished.

1653 Humphrey Moseley, a printer, registers for publication *The History of Cardenio,* which he identifies as a play by Fletcher and Shakespeare.

1728 Lewis Theobald, the author of *Shakespeare Restor'd,* releases a tragi-comedy titled *The Double Falsehood,* allegedly based on the manuscript of an unnamed play by Shakespeare. The unnamed play may be *Cardenio.*

That's all I had to go on. The play was performed, yet never published. In 1653 Humphrey Moseley obviously possessed a copy. He must have planned to print it; there could be no other reason for going to the trouble and expense of registration. But no evidence of publication exists.

Another question was why Lewis Theobald would change the title. His other so-called "improvements" to Shakespeare's plays never involved changing the original titles. If the play had been *Cardenio,* that's the title he would have used no matter how capriciously he fiddled with the plot.

While I was pondering this, the doorbell rang. I jumped up. UPS at last.

But it wasn't UPS. When I opened the door, I saw a Volkswagen Golf in my driveway and at my threshold a tall, well-built man, whom I judged to be about my own age, wearing jeans and a dark blue T-shirt. He had a mop of brown hair touched with silver at his temples. In his hand was the envelope that I had dispatched to the Arts Building. I looked from his eyes to the envelope and back.

"I'm Michael Burton."

I blinked. "Not UPS? I was expecting my books."

"Sorry." He held out the envelope. "You sent the wrong key. At least, the one to the office is wrong. The key to the Arts Building works."

"Come in." I took the envelope and looked inside. "Sorry. You have my house key."

He stepped inside just as Professor Weaver's striking clock in the hall chimed majestically. Two o'clock. Starting at the sudden sound, he laughed. *"Tempus fugit."*

"Quite," I agreed, noticing how his glance shifted from object to object in the front hall, taking in the clock, the mahogany side table and the Victorian settee, and then drifted through the double doorway into the living room, where his eyes lingered upon the marble fireplace and the bookcases. I recognize an appraising look when I see one. He had my office. Did he covet my home as well? I was prepared to hate him.

"I'm hunting for a place to live."

"Good luck," I said, my suspicion confirmed. "Have a seat while I fetch the right key."

I trotted upstairs to the study, found my key ring, and pulled off the key to the office. It was engraved, "Do not copy," as were all keys provided for faculty. I didn't know how I'd managed to put my house key in the envelope; I put it back on the ring.

Returning to the living room, I gave him the office key. "This is definitely the right one."

"Thank you."

When he did not appear ready to leave, I asked, "Would you like a cup of tea?"

"Sure, if it's not too much trouble."

"No trouble." I went into the kitchen and put on the kettle. While the water was coming to the boil, I wondered why I had offered hospitality to this usurper.

He followed me into the kitchen. "You have a nice house."

"It's not mine. I'm looking after it for Professor Weaver while he's in California."

"Archibald Weaver?"

"That's right."

"*The* Archibald Weaver?"

He couldn't have looked more reverential if we had been standing in a cathedral. I half expected him to genuflect to the refrigerator.

"His work on Plato has had a tremendous influence on my approach to literature."

"Really?" I said. "What would you like in your tea?"

"Milk."

He gazed starry-eyed at Professor Weaver's kitchen appliances until I handed him a mug and directed him back to the living room.

We sat facing each other. I wondered how much he knew about me. The way some people saw it, I was practically a child molester.

I smiled at him. "Your field is literary criticism, isn't it?" I already knew it.

"Yes."

Before I could think up another question, the doorbell rang. Saved by the bell.

"That must be UPS," I said.

He could have seized the opportunity to leave. But he waited, standing to one side with the mug of tea in his hand while the deliveryman carried in nineteen cartons of books and set them down on the living room carpet. Now there was scarcely room to turn around.

"What are you going to do with them?" Michael asked after the UPS man had left.

"I'll store Professor Weaver's books in the cartons and put my own on the shelves."

"May I help?"

"Oh, no."

"I can reach the top shelves without a chair, and I don't think you can."

At five-foot-eight, I'm tall for a woman, but Michael had six inches on me. I could have informed him that I owned a library stool, but decided not to. There were many books, and I could use a hand.

"You're very kind," I said. "I suppose I could use some assistance."

We worked in silence, clearing and then filling one shelf at a time. Michael had slender fingers that handled each book with care. Occasionally we glanced at each other. I considered inviting him to stay for dinner. I had a bottle of Chianti, a jar of spaghetti sauce and some pasta on hand. But if he accepted, I might have a problem getting rid of him before George Pinkus arrived at nine. Tight squeeze. Better not risk it.

Was Michael feeling guilty about taking my office? Or was he simply being helpful to a woman in distress? Or did he want to know me better? None of the above, I decided. From the absorbed way he inspected each volume before placing it in a carton, I deduced that his interest was in Professor Weaver's books, and not in me.

"Have you read any of these?" he asked as he placed an armful of books in a carton.

"I've glanced through a few. Plato had a profound influence on Renaissance literature, but not so much on Shakespeare – at last not directly."

"You're right, of course." Michael squatted on his heels, examining a leather-bound copy of Plato's *Symposium*. "I wonder what difference it would have made to Shakespeare's writing if he had gone to university."

"A good question," I answered.

After one hour's acquaintance, I was beginning to like Michael, usurper though he was. He had shown consideration in dropping by to get the right key instead of asking Mrs. McPherson to telephone a third time. His help with the books was making the work much easier and more pleasant. Maturity, I decided, had much to recommend it.

When the hall clock struck five, I stood up. Rubbing the small of my back with both hands to suggest a slight ache, I said, "Enough for today. I can do the rest tomorrow. Would you like a drink before you go?"

"No thanks. There are a few things I need to do at ... the office." He glanced away awkwardly.

I found myself hoping that he would offer to come back to help me the next day, for the work was barely half done.

"A pleasure to have met you," was all he said.

After he left, I worked through my e-mails. The two from Sebastian I deleted unread. For supper I ate fruit and yogurt. By eight-thirty I was ready for George.

# Five

Professor Weaver's house – my home for the time being – was on leafy, quiet Inchbury Street, one mile from the campus of Melrose University. It was a 1920's house, with a wide porch. In front of the porch was a planting of shrubs and small evergreens: bridalwreath spirea, viburnum, junipers and yews. On the porch stood a wicker swing, the size of a loveseat, with striped green-and-white canvas cushions.

I carried a glass of iced tea out to the porch and sat down on the swing to wait for George. Across the street, Harold and Alma Rogers, my octogenarian neighbours, stared from their porch. I gave them a friendly wave, expressing assurance that all was well with the world. From the beginning I had sensed their disapproval of the woman staying in Professor Weaver's house.

It was still broad daylight, though high in the maple that grew in front of the house a robin trilled its evening song. The wicker swing creaked luxuriously. What good fortune to have the use of this pleasant house on this quiet, tree-lined street! And if I decided to stay in Atherton, it would be mine for three more years. Rent free. True, I'd have to borrow against my Registered Retirement Savings Plan to meet living expenses, but it would be worth it. Three years would be enough time to prepare for *Cardenio's* restoration to the world. After that, money would never again be a problem.

Yesterday, at this same hour, I was clearing out my office. No job. No prospect of a job. No plan for the future. And then George Pinkus appeared. Saviour or devil? Only time would tell. I remembered him as a pudgy guy with body odour, an underachieving student always trying to borrow somebody's lecture notes. Why he missed so many lectures had never been clear. It wasn't as if he played sports, or worked on the student newspaper, or even sat around the Junior Common Room with the rest of us while we denounced our parents' bourgeois values, our professors' abysmal teaching skills, and the cultural stagnation of the Western World.

George struck me as stupid, but devious. Always on the lookout for opportunities to get ahead with the least possible expenditure of effort, he reminded me of a grub that feeds on trees by sucking the sap out of green twigs. But this was not an analogy I wanted to pursue too far.

"Luck happens when opportunity meets sound preparation," my father used to say. No question my preparation had been sound. Ten years of studying the evolution of Shakespeare's imagery, from the exuberant violence of *Titus Andronicus* to the faded music of *A Winter's Tale,* then a decade devoted to textual criticism. And now, at just the right moment, opportunity came knocking at the door. Not the kind of respectable once-in-a-lifetime opportunity that everybody hopes for, but one so rare that its equal might appear once in a century, if that. It was a long shot, but I must pursue it.

I'd been waiting a long time. In eleven years, I would be fifty-two, the age at which Shakespeare died. When he was my present age, he was writing plays like *King Lear, Measure for Measure* and *Macbeth*. What could I do at forty-one to justify myself? Easy question. If I could restore Shakespeare's lost play to the world, I would ask no more.

I took a sip of my iced tea. Cool and sweet, it eased the tightness of my throat.

A pair of joggers, a man and a woman, passed by, with their arms pumping and legs moving rhythmically as if battery-driven. A modern form of self-flagellation. What god did they please by pounding the pavement in thirty-degree-Celsius heat?

A mosquito buzzing around my head finally settled behind my ear. I gave a hard slap and, when I pulled my hand away, saw that the mosquito had been full of blood. Mine, no doubt. As I wiped off the smear, I saw George plod around the corner from the direction of the bus stop, casting a shadow twice the length of his body. He wore the same tweed jacket as the night before, despite the heat, and he carried a black briefcase. When he turned up the walk to the porch, I noticed a glint of metal at his wrist and realized that his briefcase was handcuffed to his wrist. He climbed the porch steps. There were beads of sweat on his forehead.

"Long walk from the bus stop," he said, pulling a grimy handkerchief from his pocket to wipe his face.

Wearing heavy tweeds and carrying fifty pounds of excess weight would make four blocks feel like a mile. Carrying my half-empty glass, I opened the front door to show him in.

Harold and Alma were watching. This chubby man with his King George V beard and shabby tweeds had a comically sinister look, like a spy in a 1940's B movie. Seeing us vanish into the house, perhaps they thought he was my lover. Christ! I hoped not.

I motioned him into the living room.

"Would you like some iced tea?"

"Just water."

"I'll only be half a minute."

By the time I returned from the kitchen, he had unlocked the handcuffs with a tiny key.

"A precaution," he said as he set them on a side table. I handed him the glass. He drank the water while standing, drank it in great, thirsty gulps, and gave the glass back to me. When he took off his jacket, I saw half-moons of sweat under the arms of his short-sleeved shirt. After returning the glass to the kitchen, I sat down on the sofa.

With a second key he unlocked his briefcase and withdrew a flat bundle wrapped in chamois leather. He set it on the coffee table and sat down beside me. I held my breath. With as much care as a mother undressing a delicate child, his stubby fingers unwrapped the manuscript.

"There you are," he said.

"Ah!"

Slowly I let out my breath. For a while I was locked into silence. So this was it. Greyish-yellow paper. Rag linen – otherwise it never would have lasted. Spiky letters in black ink, hard to decipher, written with a sharpened quill four centuries ago. The Holy Grail. I stared but could not speak.

"Are you convinced?" he asked.

"Incredible." My voice trembled. I'd seen genuine Seventeenth-Century manuscripts in the Bodleian Library at Oxford, and I'd seen forgeries too, some very clever. But science had developed sophisticated techniques to determine the age of paper, binding, glue and ink. As I examined the manuscript, I anticipated that this manuscript could pass every test.

When I leaned forward, I smelled George's sweat. He sat bunched up, defensive, while I silently read the first page.

ACT THE FIRST
SCENE I

*Enter Cardenio and Pedro.*

*Cardenio.* These seven days spent from home have now undone
My peace forever.

*Pedro.* Good, be patient, sir.

*Cardenio.* She is my wife by contract before Heaven
And all the angels, sir.

*Pedro.* I do believe you;
But where's the remedy now? Luscinda's gone.
Fernando hath possession.

*Cardenio.* There's the torment!

*Pedro.* This day, being the first of your return,
Unluckily proves the first of her fastening.
Her father holds a good opinion of the bridegroom,
As he's fair spoken, sir, and wondrous rich –

*Cardenio.* There goes the devil in a sheepskin!

*Pedro.* With all speed
They clapped it up suddenly: I cannot think, sure,
That Luscinda over-loves him; though being married,
Perhaps, for her own credit, she doth intend
Performance of an honest, duteous wife.

*Cardenio.* Sir, in this sad business, question nothing.
You will but lose your labour; 'tis not fit
For any, hardly mine own secrecy,
To know what I intend. I take my leave, sir.
I find such strange employments in myself,
That unless death pity me and lay me down,
I shall not sleep these seven years, sir.
[Exit

I paused.

"Well?" George asked. "What do you think?"

"It's good. Strong opening lines. The handling of metre sounds like Shakespeare, except for that odd repetition of 'sir.' Look at that speech. Cardenio says 'sir' three times in seven lines."

"So you have doubts?"

"Let's say I have reservations. This is not hackwork." I read the next speech aloud.

*Pedro.* That sorrow's dangerous can abide no counsel;
'Tis like a wound past cure: wrongs done to love
Strike the heart deeply; none can truly judge on't
But the poor sensible sufferer whom it racks
With unbelievèd pains, which men in health,
That enjoy love, not possibly can act,
Nay, not so much as think. In troth, I pity him.

"Oh, yes. This is Shakespeare's language," I said.

I shivered. After a silence of four hundred years, these lines of dialogue spoke again.

I looked up. "So you've held onto this manuscript for twenty years. That's a long time."

"No point rushing. As I explained last night, I needed somebody with academic credentials to present it to the world."

"In twenty years, you could have earned your own credentials."

"I had you in my sights."

That was George, always looking for someone else to do the work.

He continued: "At first I didn't know what to do with it. Reading it was murder. I gave up after the first act."

"Just as well. The less handling, the better."

I turned to the second page. Pencilled in the margin were the words: Enter Mr/Schancke. I recognized the name. John Schancke was an actor. The *First Folio* names him in a list of the principal players in Shakespeare's plays.

Pointing to this cue, I said, "What you have looks like a prompt copy of the play. Fire destroyed the Globe Theatre on June 29, 1613. The cannon that was used for special effects, such as heralding the entrance of a king, was loaded with gunpowder and wadding. The theatre's thatched roof ignited when the cannon was fired during a performance of *King Henry VIII.* The Globe burned to the ground in two hours. Until now, I had assumed that all the prompt books perished too."

I turned to the back page. The play ended with the mandatory couplet:

And in all times may this day ever prove
A day of triumph, joy, and honest love!

Beneath this couplet was the word "finis" in the same secretary hand as the text, and below that, in different handwriting:

*The History of Cardenio*
*Approved to be acted publicly*
*February 27, 1613*
*Geo Buck*

"Who was he?" George asked.

"Master of the Revels. A top bureaucrat. Before any play could be performed or published, he had to license it." I looked at George. "You should know that. It was covered in the Shakespeare course we both took."

"Unlike you, I missed a few classes."

"I remember," I said absently as I picked up the manuscript. It measured approximately eight-by-eleven inches, and it was slightly less than one inch thick. There was no cover or title page. The pages were bound so stiffly that opening them fully would have cracked the book apart.

"It can't be photocopied," I said, "unless one uses an edge platen book copier."

"A what?"

"A device that enables a book to be photocopied without fully opening the pages. But only major libraries have copiers that are equipped like that. Another option is to unbind it, but I don't have the right solvents or a properly equipped lab. So in order to have a text I can work with, I'll have to write it out in longhand, with my pen in one hand and the other holding the book sufficiently open for me to read the words."

"How long will that take?"

"Perhaps a month." Carefully I set the manuscript upon its wrapper. "I'll get right to work. I need a publishable text before I can announce my discovery."

"*Your* discovery?" His hand hovered protectively upon the brittle paper.

"Isn't that the deal we've made? I get the glory, and share half the profits with you."

"What control will I have?"

"Rather late to think about that. You have to trust me, unless you want a lawyer to draw up a contract."

"No lawyers. Nothing in writing. But to protect my own interests, I have one more condition. I want an advance."

"An advance? You talk like you're the one who'll write the book."

"One hundred thousand."

"You can't be serious."

George's eyes locked on mine. "You know this is worth millions."

"Not without my help."

George let out a loud, rather dramatic sigh as he began to rewrap *Cardenio* in the chamois. "Maybe I should look for a backer with some cash, or just sell it to the Folger Library."

"And when the Folger asks where it came from, what will you say? George, the manuscript has no provenance and you have no credentials." I heard my voice rising, but I couldn't control it. "The most you can get on your own for this play is a few thousand from a private collector who won't ask questions. To make real money, you need a scholar with an established reputation in Shakespeare studies to launch it. You've already made that point. If anybody pays anybody one hundred thousand dollars, it should be you paying me."

He put the manuscript into his briefcase and snapped it shut. "Looks like we don't have a deal after all."

George levered himself to his feet, retrieved his jacket, and thrust his arms into the sleeves. Too numb to move, I watched as he picked up the handcuffs from the coffee table, clicked one bracelet to the briefcase handle and the other to his left wrist.

"I'm staying at the Atherton Arms. If you change your mind by noon tomorrow, you can contact me there." He reached into his pocket with his free hand and pulled out a slip of paper. "Here's my cellphone number. Don't put your call through the desk."

With the slip of paper between my fingers, I followed him into the front hall. He opened the screen door, and I came right behind him onto the porch.

"You'll regret this," I said to his retreating back as he thudded down the wooden steps.

Across the street, Harold and Alma stolidly watched.

I retreated inside and slammed the door. George was teasing me like an angler playing a fish on his line. Like a fool, I had already taken the bait.

# Six

The manuscript was gone, and gone with it the chance to rescue my career. What was left to me? I could follow George's example. Help students cheat. Be a whore in the groves of academe. Make a living selling essays over the Internet. I'd seen the ads. DueNow.com, America's Most Visited Essay Site. We're Hiring!!! CLICK HERE TO APPLY FOR A WRITING POSITION.

I stood inside the front door, my thoughts whirling. The only noise was the ticking of the hall clock. Its steadiness was beginning to quiet my brain, when suddenly came a click and an ear-tingling chime that jolted me to my senses.

Ten o'clock. Pull yourself together, I told myself. Make yourself a cup of tea. I entered the kitchen, filled the kettle, and set it on the stove to heat.

The time had come for some hard thinking. George's mutterings about the Folger were sheer bluff. Of course the Folger Institute in Washington, DC, would have an interest. As the owner of seventy-nine copies of Shakespeare's *First Folio,* which was about one-third of those still in existence, the Folger had amassed the greatest collection of Shakespeare materials in the world. But George knew as well as I did that its experts would demand an explanation of how he had obtained the manuscript.

He wasn't likely to tell them that he had stolen it from the King's College Library stacks. At first I'd been amazed that he even told me. Why hadn't he invented a story? He could have claimed that the manuscript had been passed down through his family for generations. Convincing or not, such an account could not be disproved. For lack of a better, I might end up using such a lie myself.

But now I saw his cunning. To work on a stolen manuscript, knowing it stolen, would make me a criminal too. That would be George's hold over me. Possessing stolen goods and profiting from the proceeds of crime are both criminal offences. He would never need to fear my reneging on our deal. We would be in it together for better or for worse, so long as we both should live. Was that what I wanted?

I took a mug from the kitchen cupboard. It was my own mug, not one of Professor Weaver's. The lettering on the side, "English Majors are Novel Lovers," was nearly worn off. Years ago a boyfriend had given me this mug. His name was Guy. Guy Gordon. He wasn't an English major. He wasn't even a student. Just a guy named Guy whom I'd met while tree planting up north one summer. He had bought the mug for me. He was my first lover, and I suppose that was why I had kept it.

That long, hot summer Guy and I used to take walks into the woods or sit by the riverside with our feet in the cool water. We'd hide behind the trees to make love. Guy had jet-black hair. His face and neck were tanned, but when he took off his clothes his skin was so pale it reminded me of milk. The day after the tree planting ended, he went with me to the train station. It was a small station with a big railway clock. We sat on the bench in the waiting room where there was nobody else and looked at the clock. He caressed my hand and said that he would see me the next summer. We heard the rumble of my train approaching.

Guy never knew what followed. It was just too complicated. I'm sure he loved me. He would have wanted to marry me. But I was twenty years old, full of dreams that did not include him. About to enter my final year of university, I was already making plans for grad school. There's no way I could have settled for married life in a small Northern Ontario town. It would not have been fair to Guy or to me. So I dealt with my problem alone.

Thinking of Guy as I poured the boiling water into the mug, I remembered how principled I had been at twenty. If Mephistopheles had made me an offer of infinite knowledge, power and riches, I'd have sprinkled him with holy water.

I was smarter now. No more illusions. Call me Doctor Faustus. My soul was up for grabs.

I carried the mug to the living room and sank into an armchair. While sipping my tea, I reflected upon the Faust legend. It has many versions; but in every telling of the story, the devil leaves the Faust figure undisturbed to enjoy his wealth and fame for many years. Only at the end does he reappear to claim his due.

George was giving the story a modern twist. He wanted payment in advance.

The problem was: how could I get my hands on one hundred thousand dollars when my only assets were a ten-year-old BMW and a Registered Retirement Savings Plan worth sixty thousand?

Why hadn't I saved any money over the years? The reasons were sound enough. Too many student loans to pay off. Too many summers in England poring through old manuscripts in the Bodleian Library at Oxford. Too many books I couldn't resist buying. An assistant professor's salary can go only so far, and I had usually managed to spend every cent of mine.

Still, sixty thousand was a fair bit of change. George might settle for that. But then, what would I live on? I had no job. I would have no income during the years needed to authenticate the manuscript and write my book. How much could I actually afford to pay?

The hall clock chimed twelve. Midnight. The witching hour, when devils dragged Doctor Faustus to hell. The hour when Cinderella's coach turned into a pumpkin and her footmen into rats. Furry rats with naked, scaly tails. Sewer rats, like George.

My tea finished, I stood up. Where was that slip of paper with George's cellphone number? I wandered about looking, finally finding it on the hall floor.

Sitting at the telephone table, I punched the numbers. George picked up on the first ring. I got right to the point.

"George, we should talk."

"Can you get the money?"

"I'll pay ten thousand dollars."

I listened as he sucked in his breath, and then exhaled with a burst.

"You think I'd part with that manuscript for ten thousand?"

"It's more than you'll get on eBay for a stolen manuscript."

Silence.

"Hold on," George said. "I've got another call."

I waited, drumming my fingers on the telephone table. Who else could be phoning George at midnight?

The other caller was taking a long time. I was wondering whether to hang up when George came back on the line.

"Deirdre, you still there?" His voice shook.

"I'm here."

"Look. I'm willing to negotiate. But ten thousand is ridiculous."

"Okay. Give me a call if you want to make a counter offer."

I put the phone back on its cradle. What would he do? I pictured George as I had seen him in his worn tweed jacket trudging from the bus stop in the midsummer heat. No car. Not even a ten-year-old car. How long would it take for him to phone me back? If necessary, I could pay twenty thousand. Top limit.

I put out the cat, went upstairs and ran a bath, tossing a handful of perfumed salts into the steaming water. I loved these small luxuries. Were perfumed bath salts an indulgence that I would now have to forego?

Before I had soaked for two minutes, the phone rang. I pulled myself half out of the tub, then changed my mind. George could call again.

His call came at ten the next morning. I let it ring four times, while eating my yogurt, before picking up the receiver.

"I'll let you in for fifty thousand," George said.

"George, you just don't get it." I forced a laugh. "Maybe you'd better give the Folger Institute a call."

I waited. He was as likely to call the RCMP.

"Let's not play games," he spluttered. "What's the most you're prepared to pay?"

"Twenty thousand."

"Make that twenty-five."

My mind, in fast-forward, foresaw a return to reduced-price vegetables, last-day-for-sale meat, and semi-stale bread – my normal diet back in grad school.

"It's a deal," I said.

"When can you bring it to me?"

"A few days."

"I can't hang around Atherton much longer. You have till the end of the week. Don't call me until you've got the money. In cash. Fifty dollar bills."

After he had hung up, I stood with the receiver still in my hand, looking out the kitchen window at the hollyhocks blooming against the back fence.

Now what should I do? Maybe my mother could mortgage her house to help me. I doubted that she would. My academic achievements had never impressed Mom. The only thing she wanted me to produce was a baby. Mom was the homebody type, the perfect granny. To complete the picture, all she needed was a bunch of grandchildren. The lack was my fault.

My sister Sheila would have been more co-operative, or so Mom liked to think. But Sheila was dead.

Still, there was no harm in trying. I punched in her number.

"Mom," I said, beginning with small talk. "How are you?"

"Fine, apart from my arthritis. And I can't sleep nights. And the doctor says my blood pressure is high."

Not such a good beginning.

"That's too bad, Mom. I hope Dad is well?"

"He hates the nursing home, wants me to bring him home."

I clucked sympathetically and decided not to ask more questions. Better get to the point.

"Mom, I've been offered a fantastic opportunity. It's a partnership, but I have to come up with twenty-five thousand dollars."

"Are you going into business?"

"Not exactly business."

"Real estate?"

"No. It's to invest in a manuscript."

"A what?"

"A hand-written copy of a play. It's four hundred years old, and possibly by Shakespeare."

"Four hundred years old? Go to Chapters. You can buy a new one for fifteen dollars."

"This may be worth millions."

"And you want me to give you twenty-five thousand?"

"Lend, not give. You'll get your money back."

"Deirdre, if you needed it for something sensible, like a down payment on a house, I'd find a way. But not for a used book."

"Thanks, Mom. I'll remember your offer when it's time to settle down." I sighed, anticipating what came next. I'd been hearing The Speech in various forms for years.

"You're forty-one," she began. "You should have settled down years ago. By now you ought to have children in high school."

I held the receiver at arm's length – a trick to keep me from losing my cool.

After five minutes, I put the phone back to my ear.

"... and what am I supposed to tell people when they ask why a beautiful girl like you isn't married?"

"Tell them I'm a lesbian." I hung up, annoyed at myself for even trying.

The bank came next. I telephoned to make an appointment with Ms. Grantly, my bank-appointed financial advisor. Luckily for me, a cancellation made it possible for her to see me in two hours.

I pressed my Holt Renfrew suit, on the theory that it's easier to get money if you look as if you don't need it. But I didn't fool Ms. Grantly, an iron lady with pencilled brows and highly lacquered yellow hair. After presenting my prospective plan for the next three years as a sort of unpaid sabbatical, I assured her that my proposal was entirely reasonable. If the bank would lend me twenty-five thousand, I would start repayment at the end of three years. "Treat it like a student loan," I suggested.

"That's not possible."

"You do it for university students."

"The government guarantees student loans. Its reasons are political."

She tilted her blond bouffant toward the computer screen. As soon as she located my banking profile, she shook her head.

"Dr. Gunn, since you are not in a position to make payments immediately, your only option is to withdraw the funds you need from your Registered Retirement Savings Plan." She gave me a hard look. "As soon as you do that, Income Tax is due on the amount withdrawn. To obtain twenty-five thousand dollars, you will need to take out approximately thirty-five. I advise against it."

I gulped. This interview was not going the way I had hoped. But it was my money, not hers. Damn the torpedoes!

Ms. Grantly frowned her disapproval, but within ten minutes I had her assurance that the funds would be available by the end of the week.

"I want it in fifty dollar bills," I said.

Her carefully drawn eyebrows shot up, but all she said was, "Very well."

Back home, I found Socrates crouched by the front door with a headless mouse between his paws. "Mar-rar!" he announced triumphantly and picked up his prey in his jaws.

"Not in the house!" Opening the door, I blocked his way with my foot.

Socrates dropped the mouse and followed me inside. While I made coffee, he sat on the kitchen floor washing his face. His method was to lick one paw and then swipe the side of that paw across his cheek. I watched him repeat the procedure until satisfied. A cat is a wonderful creature, I reflected, complete in itself, entirely self-possessed. Socrates met my admiring gaze. In his golden orbs, I saw the soul of a panther. I liked to think that we had something in common, Socrates and I.

"Well, Socrates," I said. "I'd better phone George." Now grooming his stretched-out hind leg, the cat did not answer.

Instead of a dial tone, I heard the beeping that meant Message Waiting. Who had called? Deciding to put off George for a few minutes, I tapped in my code. Two messages had arrived while I was at the bank.

The first was from Sebastian. He sounded drunk, slurring his beautiful English vowels as he whined about unanswered e-mails and my cruel neglect. I deleted his message without hearing it to the end. Somebody ought to pick him up and wring him out. But not me. Sebastian belonged in the discard file.

Michael Burton was my second caller, announcing that he would drop by in the afternoon to lend a hand with the books. He left his office number – *my* office number – to call him back if that would not be convenient for me.

Of course it would be convenient. Ten cartons of my books were still unpacked. I could use the help. And I wouldn't mind seeing him again.

My spirits buoyed, I dialed George's number. "I'll have the money on Friday," I said.

"Cash. Remember."

"Understood. I'll bring it at noon." There was a click as he hung up.

So the deal was on. To celebrate, maybe I should allow myself a drink. I glanced up at the kitchen wall clock. The dial read 11:40. Too early.

I took an apple from the fruit bowl and paced back and forth across the kitchen floor as I ate it. Unless George pulled another trick, I would have the manuscript in my hands by the weekend. I felt as excited as a kid three days before Christmas.

I had just tossed the apple core into the trash bin when the doorbell rang. It couldn't be Michael, could it? He had said afternoon. Probably a salesman, or a pair of Jehovah's Witnesses. Since my car was parked in the driveway, I couldn't pretend not to be at home. When the bell rang a second time, I went to the door.

It was Sebastian. Swaying on the porch, he held out a bunch of pink flowers wrapped in a plastic sleeve – a $4.95 bouquet from the No Frills supermarket. Not his usual style.

"Deirdre, I love you!" His words were slurred and his breath reeked. As he lurched toward me, I reached out, stiff-armed, and pushed one palm against his chest to fend him off.

"No! I don't want to see you." I would have slammed the door in his face, but I didn't want to leave him on the porch to entertain the neighbours. I stepped outside.

Across the street, Harold emerged onto his porch and held the door open for Alma to carry out a tray. She set it down on a small table that stood between their two Muskoka chairs. On the tray were a large pitcher and two tumblers. I don't know how Alma managed to fill the tumblers without spilling, the way her eyes were riveted on

Sebastian and me as I maneuvered him over to the porch swing. His bouquet fell to the floor.

"Sit!" I said, as if he were a dog, and settled him. His head flopped back.

"I brought you flowers," he mumbled.

"Yes, that is sweet of you." Doing my best to appear courteous, I picked up the flowers. "I'll take these inside and put them in water. Then call you a taxi. You did come in a cab, didn't you?"

"Don't call a cab. I need to talk to you."

"Not now."

I felt my audience's eyes upon me. To Harold and Alma my life must be as fascinating as *Coronation Street.* Yesterday evening, a bearded man came calling. Now it was an inebriated youth. And soon Michael Burton's car would pull into my driveway.

Sebastian tried to stand up, but with one sharp push I returned him to the swing. The screen door slammed as I strode inside. A toss landed Sebastian's flowers in the kitchen sink.

By the time I came back from calling a taxi, he was asleep.

When the taxi arrived ten minutes later, I woke Sebastian. He regarded me mournfully with blood-shot eyes.

"Deirdre, you don't understand."

"Nor do I want to."

The driver helped me walk him to the curb and shove him into the back seat. After the cab had driven away, I waved to Harold and Alma.

"A student," I called out. "Occupational hazard."

I went into the kitchen, poured myself a Scotch, and prepared for Michael's visit.

# Seven

The living room was dark and restful after the heat outside. I sat in an armchair, with the ceiling fan turning gently, and sipped the smooth single malt. Sebastian's flowers, retrieved from the sink, sat in a pottery jug on the fireplace mantel. No point wasting a perfectly good bunch of flowers. They added a note of grace and colour to the room.

I surveyed the remaining unpacked cartons of my books, wondering which of them held *Don Quixote.* Miguel de Cervantes' masterpiece was first published in 1605. John Shelton had translated it from Spanish into English early in 1612. It was from that translation that Shakespeare borrowed the plot of *Cardenio.*

Years had gone by since I last read *Don Quixote.* I couldn't remember much about the Cardenio episode, except that Cardenio was a youth of noble family who went mad for love and wandered about in the mountains, where he met Don Quixote. A highly romantic story, as I recalled. As soon as I unearthed my copy of *Don Quixote,* I'd have to read it again.

When I had finished my drink, I went upstairs to put on make-up and tug a comb through my hair before Michael arrived. The face that looked back at me from the bathroom mirror wasn't too bad, all things considered. I had to be careful with foundation; if I used too much, it settled in the fine creases beside my eyes. I was putting on lipstick when the doorbell rang.

This time it was Michael. I opened the screen door and motioned him in. He was wearing khaki pants and an olive-green open-neck shirt. The colour matched his eyes, which were somewhere between brown and green. Very nice eyes.

"Hello." He gave me a tentative smile. "Have you made any progress with the books?"

"Alas, no."

"You look tired."

There was a pause. "I didn't get much sleep last night."

"I'm sorry."

"Not your fault."

"But I'm part of the problem, eh?" He coloured slightly. "I must be the last person in the world you'd want to know better."

I licked my lips. "It's not that."

"Well, I won't press you. You simply looked as if you could use some help."

"With the books."

"Of course. With the books."

He was watching me as he spoke. I forced a smile. He had a way of looking at me that I found unnerving. I was wary of him, as I tend to be of anyone who is too kind. But if Michael had an ulterior motive, it was Archibald Weaver's library, not my body, that he wanted to lay his hands on.

I waved toward the living room. "Shall we begin?"

Michael agreed that we should finish taking down Professor Weaver's books before unpacking the rest of mine.

We worked silently. As he took each volume from the shelves, he handed it to me to add to the proper pile.

When we had finished emptying the bookcases, I headed into the kitchen to find a cloth to wipe the shelves. At the doorway, I looked back. Michael was kneeling on the floor, tearing off the packing tape from a carton of my books.

I said, "Michael, if you see a copy of *Don Quixote* while you're unpacking, grab it for me."

"*Don Quixote?*" His hand, reaching for a book, stopped in mid-air. "Sure ... if I see it."

When we were unpacking the final carton, *Don Quixote* showed up.

"I haven't read this for years," Michael said, flipping the dog-eared pages.

"Neither have I."

"Any special reason to read it now?" He handed it to me.

"No," I said hastily as I set it on the coffee table. "Merely a whim. There are days when I feel rather like Don Quixote, as if I've been tilting at windmills and fighting giants all my life."

A smile spread across his face. "You're not like Don Quixote, except for being a bit too romantic."

"You've got that wrong." I refused to smile. Whatever he meant, I didn't want to hear an explanation. Too personal.

When we had finished packing Professor Weaver's books into the cartons, we lugged them to the attic. Nineteen heavy boxes. After that, I really had to offer him dinner.

"You must be hungry," I said. "I have wine, and we can order Chinese. There's an excellent place that delivers."

"Good idea."

I opened a bottle of chilled Chardonnay. When the food arrived, we ate it at the kitchen table, Socrates twining about our legs. Michael didn't object. As I watched breaded chicken balls disappear into his mouth, I wondered how he kissed. Hard? No. His lips were too full. They'd be soft, lingering kisses.

I set down my fork, too tired to feel particularly hungry, and was contemplating the potential of Michael's kisses, when he suddenly asked, "A penny for your thoughts."

"What? I don't think they're worth a penny." I felt my cheeks flush.

Michael, busily eating, did not notice.

As soon as we had finished the meal, he pushed his chair back from the table.

"I'll be on my way," he said. "I'm writing an article that I want to complete this evening."

I thanked him for his help with the books.

"Thanks for dinner," he said. "My treat next time."

"I'll look forward to that."

Neither of us suggested when next time might be. And on that note, we left it.

I put Socrates outdoors for the night and, with *Don Quixote* in my hand, climbed the stairs. I set my book on the bedside table.

What I needed was sleep. But as soon as I got into bed and switched off the bedside light, curiosity took hold.

Where in Cervantes' thousand-page novel would I uncover Cardenio's story?

Until now, I had never researched the source of a Shakespeare play before reading the play itself. But this time, doing it backwards made sense. First, I had time on my hands – two days, to be exact – before the manuscript of *Cardenio* would be mine. Second, even after receiving the manuscript, I wouldn't be able to work on the text of the play until I had transcribed it and made a usable hard copy.

The novelty of this approach appealed to me. Up to a point, I could put myself in Shakespeare's shoes and enter the story as he had entered it for the first time. I pictured Will Shakespeare on his way home from a performance at the Globe Theatre. The year is 1612. Passing by a bookseller's stall, he sees a new book on display. It's *Don Quixote,* by Miguel de Cervantes, the popular Spanish writer, translated into English for the first time. "Ah!" says Shakespeare as he picks it up. "I've been wanting to read this." He buys it, takes it home. After pouring a cup of claret, he lights a candle, settles into a comfortable chair, and opens the book.

Instead of helping me to drop off to sleep, this imaginary scenario woke me up completely. I wanted to read for myself what Shakespeare had read.

I sat up, turned on the light, and picked up *Don Quixote.* Having no idea where to find the Cardenio episode, I began at the beginning. Before finding what I was looking for, I had followed the melancholy knight's adventures for twenty-four chapters.

By then I was wide awake.

In the wild mountains of the Sierra Morena, Don Quixote and his squire Sancho Panza find a battered travelling case lying beside a trail. In the case is a diary. This is not an ordinary diary, for its pages are filled with anguished poetry upon two themes – the faithlessness of a certain woman and the writer's betrayal by a trusted friend.

While Don Quixote is reading the diary, a stranger enters. It is Cardenio, the diarist himself. Bearded and half-naked, he leaps like a mountain goat from crag to crag. Don Quixote soon learns that Cardenio is a perfect gentleman when in his right mind, but a homicidal maniac whenever a fit of madness strikes. In a lucid interval, he offers to tell his story, but on the condition that no one interrupt. Don Quixote agrees.

I reached for my pen:

Setting: Andalusia and Spain [separate countries then]

Main Characters: Cardenio, Luscinda, and Fernando

- Cardenio and Luscinda have exchanged secret vows committing them to each other.
- Luscinda has asked Cardenio to ask his father to ask her father for her hand in marriage. [The proper way to do it, back then]
- Cardenio doesn't do it, because he knows that his father does not want him to marry yet.
- Cardenio's father arranges for him to enter the household of Duke Ricardo, a Grandee of Spain, as a companion for the Duke's elder son.
- Full of sorrow at leaving Luscinda, Cardenio journeys to Duke Ricardo's estate, where he

becomes a close friend of the Duke's younger son, Fernando. Fernando, like Cardenio, is secretly betrothed.

- When the two young men visit Cardenio's home in Andalusia, Cardenio allows Fernando a glimpse of Luscinda.
- Smitten with Luscinda's beauty, Fernando vows to marry her.

At this point in the story, Don Quixote forgets his promise not to interrupt. Flying into a fit of madness, Cardenio runs away.

I yawned as I closed the book. So far, one big yawn was all the story was worth. Switching off my bedside lamp, I trusted that the play would be better than the book. Shakespeare always improved on his sources. No matter how feeble the original, the Bard would work his usual magic.

Outside the open window, two tomcats yowled. One was Socrates, defending his territory against his arch-enemy, a big ginger cat. A female was involved. In the morning I'd likely be doctoring a torn ear and rubbing antiseptic on dirty scratches.

I covered my head with a pillow to deaden the caterwauling. Professor Weaver should have had Socrates neutered. The world is overpopulated with unwanted cats. Unwanted people too. Maybe we'd all be better off neutered. Cardenio's life would be less complicated. So would mine. Sebastian's too. Michael I would spare for now; as an intact male he had potential. As for George Pinkus, what difference would it make?

Friday it rained, not a good pelting rain to cleanse the muggy air, but a steamy drizzle that would stop for a while and then start again. Socrates refused to go outside. Presumably he had lost the fight. After cleaning a gash on his chest, I showered and inspected my clothes closet for the right thing to wear.

For my visit to George's hotel room, I needed something casual, yet professional enough to make clear that I was the person in charge. A crisp linen dress would do nicely, I decided, tan with white details. I did my make-up carefully and then left for the bank, carrying my empty briefcase. It was dark brown, with contrasting stitching that gave it a slightly sporty look. My initials were embossed in gold.

As I drove downtown with my car's windshield wipers swishing back and forth, I realized that I should have brought an umbrella. Handcuffs would have been a good idea too. Maybe George looked ridiculous with his briefcase manacled to his wrist, but imagine what would happen if a couple of punks targeted me as I came out of the bank. Wouldn't they get a surprise to discover twenty-five thousand dollars in my briefcase!

Pulling into the municipal parking lot halfway between the bank and the Atherton Arms, I sat in the car for five minutes, willing myself to venture into the dripping rain. My choice of dress had been a mistake; nothing wrinkles faster than wet linen. The time was already 11:30 when I opened the car door and stepped into a puddle.

The bank had the money ready. No one attacked me during my two-block walk from the bank to the Atherton Arms. Without incident, I passed through the revolving glass door into the lobby.

From the twenty-foot ceiling an enormous chandelier hung suspended, as if to remind visitors of past glory. With its dozens of crystal prisms, the chandelier could still look magnificent, if someone would simply clean it. How long had it been since the last time?

In the days of King Edward VII, the Atherton Arms had been the town's premier hotel – the Park Plaza of its day. A century past its prime, it was not quite a fleabag, but sliding perilously close. The perfect habitat for George. The right setting for all manner of shady deals.

The lobby reeked of stale tobacco. Considering that Atherton had banned smoking in public places one year earlier, those odours must have thoroughly permeated the threadbare carpets and the shabby upholstered chairs.

On a tall stool behind the counter sat the desk clerk, a middle-aged man wearing a green short-sleeved shirt, blue suspenders, and a string tie. He had one of those piggy faces – round with watery blue eyes, a snub nose, and receding chin. His sparse hair was combed across his scalp and oiled into place. At his back stood a wall of mostly empty pigeonholes.

"Hello. What can I do for you?"

I pushed my fingers through my wet, flattened hair. "I've come to see one of your guests, Mr. George Pinkus."

Before I could say more, the telephone rang and the clerk picked up the receiver.

"Atherton Arms." A pause. "Yeah, we got a vacancy. Thirty dollars per night." Another pause. "That's the cheapest we got." A third pause. "One double bed." The desk clerk scratched his chin. "Sure you can. But I need a major credit card to hold it for you." I could faintly hear the caller's voice, but not his words. The desk clerk rolled his eyes. "No. That's the rule, and I can't change it. Sorry." He set down the receiver and returned his watery gaze to me.

"I don't know Mr. Pinkus' room number," I continued. "Could you ring and tell him his visitor is here?"

"Name?"

I balked at this, as if giving my name would admit a connection between me and this sleazy place.

"He'll know who it is."

"I have to give him your name."

"Deirdre Gunn."

The desk clerk rang George.

"Your friend says, go right up. Room 312. Third floor. You have to take the stairs."

Inwardly protesting that George was not my friend, I crossed the lobby. In crudely drawn letters a cardboard sign announced that the elevator was out of service. I marched up the stairs. In the hallway leading to Room 312, half the light bulbs in the wall sconces were burned out.

At my knock, George opened the door. He was wearing the same tweed jacket as before. He leaned out from his doorway, glancing quickly up and down the hall.

"Come in." He closed the door behind us and locked it.

With one quick look I took in the room. Beige walls. TV on a stand. Small clock radio on the bedside table. The usual furniture. A running toilet in the bathroom. George's open suitcase lay on the bed. Goose bumps crawled up my arms at the sight of his blue striped pyjamas and his dingy underwear.

"I'm packing," he said. "I'll take the bus back to Toronto as soon as you and I have settled our affairs."

"'Settling affairs' sounds sordid."

"Call it what you like."

"I've brought the money. Give me the manuscript and I'll leave you to your packing."

I kept my eyes on George as he took his briefcase from the shelf above the clothes rack.

"First, the money," he said.

Opening my briefcase, I set the neat pink packs of fifty-dollar bills on the dresser.

His hands shook as he counted the bills in the first pack. He flipped through the other packs, then measured them by pressing down each one to be sure it was just as thick as the one he had counted. There were beads of perspiration on his forehead. I smelled his sweat.

"That seems correct." He took out *Cardenio,* still swathed in chamois, from his briefcase.

I unwrapped the soft leather and allowed my fingers to brush the manuscript's brownish, faded ink. It was mine.

"Give me your phone number and e-mail address," I said. "It will take a couple of weeks to make a longhand copy. I'll get in touch when it's done."

He gave me his card: "George Pinkus. Professional Tutoring." I shoved it into my handbag, picked up my briefcase, and turned toward the door. My hand was on the knob.

"Don't call me unless there's an emergency," he said. "I'll do the phoning."

"All right." I couldn't imagine what kind of emergency he meant. If I had not been so desperate to get out of this dingy room and down-at-the-heels hotel, I might have asked.

I turned the knob and left. The lock clicked behind me.

In the lobby, I avoided looking at the desk clerk as I passed the counter on my way out.

The rain had stopped. Through a rift in the clouds, sunshine slanted downward in a shaft of watery light. As I walked back to the parking lot in my soggy linen dress, I could hear angels singing the *Hallelujah Chorus* in my mind.

I clutched the handle of my briefcase with all my might, and locked the car doors as soon as I was inside. My briefcase lay on the passenger's seat beside me. At every red light, I laid my hand protectively upon it until the light turned green. I drove straight home.

# Eight

A local murder is front-page news. It was the big story in the next day's *Atherton Advocate.* "Toronto man found slain in hotel room." The police had released few details. Their statement said they had several leads.

One of those leads led to me. As Police Detective Robert Agnew informed me, George Pinkus' address book listed only two Atherton residents, and one of them was Deirdre Gunn. Sitting stiffly in a leather armchair in my living room, he stared at me across the coffee table with hard eyes that looked as if they had seen it all before.

"Who was the second?" I asked.

"I can't give you that information."

I hadn't expected him to, but no harm in asking.

Detective Agnew shifted in his chair, which creaked under his weight. He was a large man, about fifty, with a grey brush cut and a deeply creased brow. He had probably spent a quarter of a century grilling suspects, though at this point he wasn't exactly grilling me. Nor was I a suspect – I hoped.

Agnew's assistant, Constable Debbie Montour, a dark-haired young woman with coppery skin, had grabbed a dining room chair, where she sat hunched over a notebook. Every time I opened my mouth, she scribbled ferociously, writing ten words for every one I uttered. What could she possibly be writing about? My body language?

I returned the detective's stare.

"How were you connected with Mr. Pinkus?" he asked.

"I wasn't."

"You mean you didn't know him?"

"We were classmates at university twenty years ago. I hadn't seen him since."

Agnew's eyes narrowed as he leaned toward me. "Until he came to Atherton to see you."

I cleared my throat. "I doubt his purpose was to see me."

"But he did see you."

"He dropped into my office, yes."

"At night."

"Yes."

"Wasn't that unusual? Why didn't he visit during normal hours, when other people would be in the building?"

Agnew's tone made me nervous. I couldn't reveal the reason George wanted to see me alone. If he knew about our arrangement, he would know that I had a motive for murder.

Cold sweat formed on my brow. My tongue felt stiff and thick. Constable Montour kept on writing, pausing only to brush back a lock of straight black hair that had escaped from the bun at the back of her neck. She was in uniform. Agnew wasn't.

"George was in town on some business of his own. I don't know what it was. He thought he'd look me up."

"At your office." Agnew's voice dripped with disbelief.

"He didn't know my home address." At least that was true.

"All he knew was that you were a member of the English Department at Melrose?"

"Yes."

"You still haven't told me why he came to see you at night."

"I believe he didn't arrive in town until after normal office hours."

"In that case, why didn't he wait till morning?"

"It was my last day on faculty. I was clearing my office. He wouldn't have found me there the next day."

"Because you'd been fired."

Constable Montour raised her pen expectantly.

I squirmed. "Not at all. I was on a two-year contract, and it expired. That's all."

"So George Pinkus dropped by your office at night to say hello. He went to all that trouble, even though his purpose in coming to Atherton was not to see you?"

"You've got it."

"Did you see him again?"

Now I was sweating all over. No point in denial. Harold and Alma had seen the man with the George V beard when he entered my home and when he left. I didn't know whether their hearing was sharp enough to catch my parting words, but if they did, "You'll regret this" certainly sounded incriminating. They wouldn't forget.

"He came to my home the next evening. I had invited him for a drink."

"And you talked ... about old times?"

That slight pause rattled me. He slowly leaned back and crossed one leg over the other. Constable Montour scribbled feverishly.

"Old times, yes. News about people we both knew … friends in common."

"But you and the deceased did not part as friends, did you?"

The constable's ballpoint hung in midair.

"Not on friendly terms. That's true."

"What did you quarrel about?"

"After four or five drinks, who knows?"

"So you and Mr. Pinkus got drunk and had a fight?"

"You make it sound like a barroom brawl."

"That's your suggestion, not mine. According to witnesses, you appeared to threaten him. The witnesses did not mention Mr. Pinkus staggering or weaving, although they were observant of other details. They noticed that he wore a tweed jacket, even though the night was warm. Thirty-degree heat, in fact. They also observed that he carried a briefcase." The detective uncrossed his legs and leaned forward, his eyes boring into mine. "Funny that he brought his briefcase on a social call. What did he have in it?"

"How would I know?"

"Pictures, maybe?"

"Pictures?"

"You're a player, aren't you?"

"A what?"

"Lots of lovers? Maybe you like to pose for your boyfriends?"

I felt the blood drain from my face. What was he saying? That George's briefcase held incriminating photographs of me?

"I've interviewed university officials," he said. "I know why Melrose didn't want to keep you. Also, I know about the number of men who come and go at your home. Last Thursday, there were two in one afternoon."

"That hardly sounds like Union Station."

"Maybe not, but it leaves you extremely open to blackmail."

I drew in a long, slow breath. I don't know what Agnew expected me to say. But for me, the truth dawned at that moment. He was barking up the wrong tree, and the smart move was to let him.

Let him believe in non-existent pornographic pictures. Let him pursue that theory as long as he liked. It would lead nowhere. By the time he realized that I had no motive for blackmail, the real killer would be found.

"You're smiling." Agnew's words startled me.

"Was I?"

"Do you find murder amusing?"

"Of course not."

He folded his arms, apparently waiting for me to say something. I had no intention of helping him along. Sitting back on the sofa, I began to relax. I thought the worst was over. I was wrong.

"Did you know Pinkus had a criminal record?" Agnew asked.

"What?"

"He spent four years in prison for molesting young boys. He tutored children with learning disabilities. Private pupils. Parents paid handsomely to have their kids' reading skills improved. Pinkus abused thirty victims over a five-year period."

"I never heard about this before."

"But you had a similar problem – a student complaint about sexual harassment."

I stared at him slack-jawed. "The student in question was twenty-two years old, not twelve."

"We've learned a lot recently about pedophile networks," he said, totally ignoring the point I had made. "Priests, choirmasters, teachers, hockey coaches ..."

"This is ridiculous. How could you possibly link me to something like that?"

"Then you'd better explain why your name was in George Pinkus' little black book." Agnew's eyes didn't flicker.

"I don't know why."

"Don't you, Deirdre?"

I stiffened. Why did he call me by my first name? Not to be friendly. The familiarity diminished me, caught me off balance. I wasn't ready to counter his next question.

"Why did you visit his hotel room?"

Constable Montour's hand paused in the air, as if she were aiming to swat a fly.

What could I say? No sense denying I was there. The desk clerk had seen me, talked to me. There had been nothing suspicious about my behaviour. If my actions had demonstrated anything, it would be my innocence. What murderer would stop at the front desk, give her name, and ask for her intended victim's room number?

"Well?" Agnew was waiting.

"I had to return something. His wallet. I found it between my sofa cushions."

"Three days after he visited your home? You're saying Pinkus was without his wallet for three days?"

"That's right."

"And he didn't phone you earlier to ask about it?"

"He thought he'd lost it somewhere else." I began to relax again. This was plausible, and who could contradict me? "I found his wallet when I was vacuuming the living room. I knew he was staying at the Atherton Arms, so I gave him a call. He doesn't have a car, and I was going downtown anyway. It was easy for me to drop it off."

"What time of day was this?"

"About noon on Friday. You must know that if you've spoken with the desk clerk."

"That's right. We do know about it. Pinkus had asked to delay his checkout because he was waiting for a visitor. The desk clerk told him he could keep the room until one o'clock. When he hadn't checked out by two, the clerk phoned his room. No answer. So he sent a maid to investigate." Agnew leaned forward. "You were the last person to see George Pinkus alive."

"Not quite."

"Meaning what?"

"The killer saw him last, not me."

Detective Agnew gave me a look that said: don't play wise with me. He stood up. When he reached into his pocket,

I half expected him to pull out a set of handcuffs. But it was just his keys.

Constable Montour put her pen and notebook into a small leather case.

"That's all for now," Agnew said. "If you're planning to leave town for any reason, call the police station first. We have to know where to find you."

# Nine

My knees felt like noodles as I wobbled into the kitchen to pour myself a Scotch. It was only 11:30 in the morning. Here I was, breaking my own rule.

While I sat at the kitchen table sipping the smooth malt, I tried to work out the implications of George's death. For the man himself, I couldn't wring out one drop of sympathy, and certainly no regret.

The killer had done me a huge favour. If he had my twenty-five thousand dollars, he was welcome to it. When I thought of the money George's death was going to save me over the years, twenty-five thousand was a pittance. No need now to share the proceeds of either the manuscript or my research. Not only the glory but also the entire profit would be mine.

Under the circumstances, it might be prudent to postpone my edition of *Cardenio* until the murderer was behind bars. Delay would not diminish its value. Unfortunately, I might have to wait longer for my rewards, but when they came, they would be mine alone.

It was too early to celebrate. Not when Detective Agnew was hunting for a suspect and seemed to have his sights on me. His suggestion for a motive was preposterous. Yet judging from the number of wrongly convicted people whose stories appear on the news nearly every day, the police are not always particular about whom they target, so long as they can make an arrest. I was certain that on the evidence, no jury of reasonable men and women could convict me of murder. But anything can happen once a trial gets rolling. Even if I were acquitted, the experience would be appalling, and I would never be able to live down such public exposure of my private life.

Who was the killer, and what was he after? If I were a detective, I'd be suspicious about that pig-faced desk clerk. He saw me enter. He knew where I was going. He saw me leave. Maybe he was in league with the killer. He could have signalled to an accomplice the moment that I left the hotel, told him the coast was clear.

I pictured a shadowy figure lurking in the corridor, knocking on the door of George's room. But what happened after the door opened was beyond my power to imagine. Agnew had not told me how George died. Had he been shot? Stabbed? Strangled? If you're a suspect, it's only reasonable to be curious about details like the murder weapon you are supposed to have used.

I got up from the table, rinsed my glass under the tap, and as I wiped it dry, wondered about the second Atherton name listed in George's address book. Whom else in this small city had George known? Man or woman? Friend or enemy? A lover? Had George Pinkus been the victim of a crime of passion? Improbable. Grotesque.

What had the killer wanted? No one except George knew that I would bring twenty-five thousand dollars in cash to his room at twelve noon. Unless he told someone. Only an idiot would blab about something like that.

But suppose he was drunk. Liquor can make a person incredibly indiscreet. Suppose he had invited somebody back to his hotel for a few drinks, or for sex, and couldn't resist bragging about his good fortune. Possible? Yes. Plausible? No.

On the other hand, perhaps it was the manuscript, not the money, that the killer wanted. Just as unlikely, and for a similar reason. George had clearly implied that I was the only person, apart from him, who knew about it. It was our secret. Having chosen me to restore Shakespeare's lost play to the world, there was no reason for him to tell anyone else. To do so would have brought no advantage. It would only have increased his risk.

If it wasn't money or the manuscript, then what was the killer after? Vengeance? One of those boys whom George abused might have wanted to even the score. A helpless twelve-year-old could not do much. But after four years of brooding, a youth of sixteen might be capable of murder.

Or it could be a parent, a father or mother who viewed George's prison term as insufficient punishment. I wished I knew the name of that second Atherton contact in George's address book. Hopefully, Detective Agnew was taking a serious look at that person too.

How much did Agnew know? Not much, or he wouldn't be dreaming up motives like blackmail. No point telling him the truth. In his eyes I'd still be a suspect. All he'd have to change was his theory about my motive. In place of "compromising photographs," he would substitute "rare manuscript." It would suit him just as well.

So this was my predicament. I had possession of the manuscript, but for the present could do nothing with it. That being the case, maybe I should put it in a safe place. But where? Shove it under my bed? Stuff it in the linen cupboard between a couple of blankets? Tear up Professor Weaver's floorboards to find a space? Every hiding place I could think of sounded futile, if not ridiculous. If the police searched my home and found *Cardenio,* the very fact that I had hidden it would raise questions. If Agnew should also learn about the twenty-five thousand dollars withdrawn from my RRSP, I'd be in real trouble.

For the present, the best place for *Cardenio* was my safety deposit box at the bank. Nothing suspicious about that. People kept all sorts of documents and old records in safety deposit boxes. That was the up side. The down side would be lack of access. How could I work on a manuscript locked up in a bank vault? Well, I couldn't.

Until Agnew forgot about me as a suspect, I would concentrate on the source, the story Cervantes tells in *Don Quixote.* Transcribing the manuscript would have to wait.

The next day was Wednesday. I went to the bank in the morning. After signing in, I placed the manuscript in my safety deposit box, and then I returned home to continue with the next installment of the story.

With *Don Quixote* and my pad of yellow paper in hand, I settled in the small armchair by my bedroom window, found the place where I had left off, and skimmed ahead.

Notes on Episode 2

- A man's voice in the wilderness. Singing. Reciting poetry. Sighing. Sobbing. Cardenio reappears, ready to resume his story.
- Nothing has changed. Despite Luscinda's urgings, Cardenio has still not worked up the courage to ask his father to ask her father for her hand.
- Poor, innocent Cardenio tells Fernando about his problem, not knowing that Fernando wants Luscinda for himself. Fernando seizes the opportunity. He offers to have a word with Cardenio's father. Cardenio accepts the offer, hoping that Fernando can persuade his father to allow the marriage.
- Sending Cardenio on a fool's errand, Fernando gets him out of town for long enough to work out his own marriage settlement with Luscinda's father.
- Cardenio receives an urgent message from Luscinda. Her wedding to Fernando will take place in two days unless Cardenio rescues her. Showing the first sign of life so far, he sets off at once.
- He arrives on the wedding day. Arrayed in jewels and finery, Luscinda is dressed for the marriage ceremony. Cardenio speaks to her through the grating of her window. She tells him that she has a dagger with which she will stab herself rather than become Fernando's wife. Cardenio replies that if she has a dagger, he has a sword.

- But does he rush to her rescue? Not Cardenio. Hiding behind a tapestry, he peeps out to watch Luscinda and Fernando exchange their marriage vows. When Fernando kisses Luscinda, she faints.
- Luscinda's mother retrieves a letter from Luscinda's bodice. Fernando snatches the letter. He reads it.
- Not waiting to learn what will happen next, Cardenio sneaks out from behind the tapestry when no one is looking. Distraught and heart-broken, he runs away to the mountains of the Sierra Morena, where he goes mad with grief.

Thus ends the second episode. Some lover! Some hero! How could even Shakespeare create sympathy for such a loser?

Before I could face the next installment, the telephone rang. It was Michael Burton, inviting me out for dinner. Well, why not? It would be a pleasure to take a break from Cardenio's misery. I could use a good meal and some attractive male company.

"Delighted," I said.

"There's a new Greek place on River Street. Somebody said it was good."

"I haven't been there." Nor had I been anywhere else, recently. For weeks I'd been a recluse, avoiding public places and curious stares. Everyone knew the university was investigating me for professional misconduct. In a small city there are no secrets. Now it was a relief to have the matter closed. Going out for dinner was a normal, social activity. I welcomed the chance.

The Minos Restaurant was a long narrow room blessed with modern air conditioning, but not overly chilled. The balmy smell of Greek coffee hung in the air. The taped background music was Greek – a husky-voiced contralto accompanied by one of those twangy guitars called a bouzouki. Michael and I sat at a small table covered with a white tablecloth. There was a single candle on our table, and daisies in a ceramic pitcher decorated with dancing nymphs pursued by Dionysus.

Michael ordered a bottle of Retsina. The stuff tasted more like turpentine than wine. But what a kick! We both chose the boiled octopus entrée. Very ethnic. After a glass of wine, I was feeling comfortable until, following some chit-chat about trends in literary criticism, the talk got personal.

"Tell me about Sebastian," Michael said as he speared a tentacle with his fork.

"Pardon?"

His question wasn't just unexpected; it was rude. It chilled the pleasant feelings I was beginning to have about Michael. But I bit my tongue. Why let my annoyance spoil my evening?

"Nothing to tell," I said calmly, keeping my tone light.

"But he must have meant a lot to you, for you to have risked your career."

His interest made me defensive. Why should I have to explain anything about my life? I chewed vigorously, grateful for the octopus's rubbery toughness that gave me time to review my answer.

"He was an addiction," I said at last, "like smoking. I've given that up too."

Michael studied me gravely. "Don't be too hard on yourself. You made a mistake."

"Maybe," I said, unimpressed by this expression of sympathy.

"Who hasn't made mistakes, especially when it comes to personal relationships? When I was fourteen, I loved my hockey coach, and he loved me."

I stopped chewing.

"He loved me so much that he spent three years in prison to pay for it. My father was terrified I'd turn out to be homosexual, especially when I wanted to study literature instead of engineering. As for my mother, she drove me nuts dropping hints that she'd always love me whatever lifestyle I chose."

"But you're not gay, are you?" I tried to sound indifferent.

"No. I turned out more or less heterosexual. I was even married for a while." He refilled my wineglass. "Would you mind if I were gay?"

"Not in the slightest," I said too quickly. Looking down at my plate, I prodded a chunk of rubbery pink flesh while reconsidering. "Michael, I'm not homophobic, but in your case I would regard it as a terrible waste."

For the next couple of minutes I concentrated on the octopus. When I looked up, I saw his eyes fixed on my face. By candlelight his eyes looked more green than brown. He leaned toward me and reached for my hand. "Nothing should ever go to waste."

I let my hand rest in his fingers.

So much for my resolve to avoid entanglements.

As we left the restaurant, Michael took my hand, and we slipped into a night that was as warm as an embrace. Turning off River Street, we left Atherton's downtown and made our way through a neighbourhood of homes, lawns and gardens. The velvety air smelled of lilies and roses. The leaves of the trees lining the streets rustled in the faint breeze. I looked up and saw a haze of tiny moths dancing in the glow of a streetlight. We passed gardens covered in shadows, and an empty schoolyard bathed in moonlight. Neither of us spoke.

A man with a beagle on a leash walked toward us on the other side of the street. A car drove by. We were not entirely alone after all.

We reached the house on Inchbury Street and closed the front door behind us; now we were entirely alone. Michael and I stood facing each other, inches apart but not touching.

I made one last attempt. "It's too soon."

"Why?"

The way he was standing with his back to the hall clock, I could see the hands pointing to 9:28 and the gothic letters that warned, *Tempus Fugit.* We were so close that one small step forward would make our bodies meet. I don't recall which of us took that step, but all at once his face was in my hair and my arms were around his back. He was taller than Sebastian; his shoulders were broader, his arms heavier. He smelled like sandalwood. I was breathless and dizzy and had to lean against him for a moment before I could lead him into the living room.

He drew me down onto the Persian carpet in front of the fireplace. He unbuttoned my blouse, unfastened my brassiere, and covered my breasts with his hands. Easily, quickly we shed our clothes. I shivered at the first touch of skin on skin, and pressed his tongue with my tongue as he pushed himself inside me.

When it was over, I opened a bottle of Merlot, which we shared while lolling naked on the leather sofa. Michael's love talk was lyrical and literary. My breasts, he told me, were like two young roes that feed amongst the lilies.

"That's from The Song of Solomon," I laughed.

"That's right. My mother gave me a Bible at my First Communion, told me to read it every day. When I got to the Song of Solomon, I went no further. But I did as she said and read it every day. I was thirteen. The world's best erotic poetry is in that Book. I know it almost by heart."

"Solomon had plenty of experience, as I recall."

"The Bible says 'threescore queens, fourscore concubines, and virgins without number.' Solomon had a way with women. Though I'm puzzled why any girl would be flattered to hear her nose compared to the Tower of Lebanon and her hair to a flock of goats."

We pulled a Bible from the bookshelves, read the choicer bits to each other, and then made love again. Michael had a firm, strong body – flat stomach, slim hips – though I would not normally have described his belly as "bright ivory overlaid with sapphires."

I took his penis in my hand – an action with foreseeable results. "Now this is more like the Tower of Lebanon," I said. My metaphor inspired him to new heights, with the result that I opened to him (to use the Biblical phrase), and he fed among the lilies of my garden.

Eventually we found our way upstairs to bed. Once during the night I woke with a start when Socrates jumped on my neck. Damn cat! I threw him off the bed, annoyed with myself for having forgotten to put him outside.

In the morning Socrates was back, lying on the pillow between our heads. His yellow eyes regarded me knowingly.

Socrates purred while Michael slept. With one arm bent under his neck and his brown hair mussed, my new lover looked as if his head belonged on my pillow. Maybe he sensed my eyes on him, because his eyelids twitched and then he woke up. Tossing Socrates onto the floor again, I rolled over into Michael's arms. Lying there with my head tucked under his chin, I was ready to admit that I wanted something permanent. Not necessarily a husband, but a husband if necessary.

"Deirdre," he said gently, "I have to leave."

"Not yet." I glanced at the clock on my bedside table. I kissed his neck, laid my hand on his stomach. "It's only seven."

"I have a meeting at nine."

A moment later I was watching his beautiful butt disappear down the hall. When he came back, he was dressed. I was still in bed. He walked over to the window and opened the drapes. Sunlight fell upon my pad of yellow paper, which still lay on the table by the armchair where I had been writing my notes.

"What's this?" He picked it up.

"Nothing. Just some scribbles for an article I'm writing."

He read aloud: " ... does he rush to her rescue? Not Cardenio. He hides behind a tapestry and peeps out to watch Luscinda and Fernando exchange their marriage vows. When Fernando kisses Luscinda, she faints. Luscinda's mother retrieves a letter from Luscinda's bodice. Fernando snatches the letter. He reads it. Not waiting to learn what will happen next, Cardenio sneaks out from behind the tapestry when no one is looking. Distraught and heart-broken, he runs away to the mountains of the Sierra Morena, where he goes mad with grief."

Michael laughed. "Somewhat melodramatic."

"Put it down," I snapped.

"Sorry." He slid a sideways glance at me as he dropped it on the table. "It didn't look confidential."

I sat up, forced a laugh. "It's not confidential. I'm the one who should apologize. It's just that ... well, I hate anybody seeing anything I write before it's finished."

He walked over to the bed, cupped my face in his hands. "Not worth a quarrel, is it? I'll give you a call."

After he left, I thumped the pillow with my fist and felt like a fool.

# Ten

I was on edge. I wanted to call Michael. Twice I picked up the phone, but I couldn't think of what to say.

I tidied the living room, and then stripped my bed and took the sheets down to the basement for laundering. I dumped them into the washer and turned it on.

Then I went up to my bedroom to make some progress with the Cardenio story. It must have been about ten when I settled in my chair by the open window. The world outside, partly hidden by green leaves, basked in morning sunshine. Peaceful Inchbury Street. If only I could lose myself in such serenity!

If I had been more circumspect in my private life, I too might now be the owner of a comfortable home on a pleasant street like this. At forty-one, I should be a full professor, secure in tenure, respected in the community.

Yet here I was, not only jobless, but a murder suspect. With my intelligence and education, how could I have got myself into such a predicament? To have worked so hard, and then to have thrown everything away! Maybe it happened because there was nothing to anchor me. I had always avoided relationships that might lead to commitment, living by the old saying, "He [better make that, *she*] travels farthest who travels alone." And just how far had I travelled? The answer put me to shame.

The rules weren't fair. But I had known from the start what they were. In my way, I had been a rebel. As long as my scholarship was impeccable, I told myself, nobody had a right to pass judgment on my personal life. As Pierre Trudeau might have said, the University Senate has no place in the bedrooms of faculty members. Try telling that to Dr. McBroom and his Presbyterian henchmen!

I picked up my copy of *Don Quixote,* thinking how well Cervantes understood dreamers who had lost their way. With a sigh, I turned to the page where I had left off, and there I found Cardenio still raging madly among the mountains of the Sierra Morena. I skimmed several chapters, wondering what would happen next. The action was so slow that I began to wonder whether Cervantes had lost interest and abandoned the tale.

After reading two more chapters, I closed the book and started downstairs to put the bedsheets in the dryer. I had reached the front hall when I heard the slam of a car door. A few seconds later, footsteps thumped up the wooden porch steps, and then the doorbell rang.

When I opened the door, there was Detective Robert Agnew, this time in uniform, waving a sheet of paper in my face. Looking past his big shoulders, I saw two police vehicles, a cruiser and a van, at the curb. The van's engine was still running. The two male officers in the van had their heads lowered as if they were reading something. There was no one in the cruiser; Agnew must have driven here on his own.

Him again, I thought, directing a cold stare at Agnew's sweating face. And why the van?

Across the street, living room curtains twitched. That would be Alma Rogers, curious to see whether the police were about to drag her scandalous neighbour off to jail.

"Good morning, Detective Agnew," I said. "More questions?"

"I have a warrant to search the premises." He thrust the paper at me, at the same time reciting the form of words, which he obviously knew by heart. "I, Robert Agnew, of the Atherton Police Force, do make oath and solemnly swear that the following is true to the best of my knowledge – "

"Never mind. I can read," I interrupted. A disappointed expression crossed his face. Obviously he enjoyed this part of the job.

I glanced down the page. The warrant set forth clearly the purpose and the terms of the search, identifying the premises at 194 Inchbury Street, the garage, the garden and also my car as subject to it. What the police were looking for was a black briefcase last seen in the possession of George Pinkus, deceased.

I gulped.

"George's briefcase?" I looked up "Is it missing?" Well, obviously it must be, or the police would not be looking for it.

I read the warrant all the way through. A judge had signed it. No doubt the entire weight of the Canadian justice system was behind it. I sighed. "You won't find the briefcase here."

"Produce it for us, and we won't need to search."

"Oh, go ahead. Do your search. Maybe that will convince you I don't have it."

"But you know where it is."

"If I knew where it was, I would tell you."

"Did you see it when you visited Pinkus' hotel room?"

"As a matter of fact, I did."

He looked at me closely, as if waiting for more.

"George was packing to go back to Toronto. I remember him lifting his briefcase down from the shelf."

"What was in it?"

"How would I know?"

Agnew kept looking, looking in the most unsettling way. I felt my cheeks burning. It was a relief to see the two uniformed officers step out of the van.

They approached single file up the concrete walk from the curb. The officer in front was fiftyish, a burly man with salt-and-pepper hair, who strode with his shoulders back, like a soldier. The other, slightly younger, was tall and thin with receding brown hair and a slight stoop. He carried a toolbox.

When they reached me, where I stood inside at the open door, Agnew introduced the shorter man as Sergeant Ivan Davis and the taller as Constable Milo Clapton. I wondered whether they would offer to shake my hand. They didn't, nor did they smile.

I was tempted to say that they would be just as far ahead going over to Tim Hortons for a coffee and leaving me to deal with Cervantes and laundry. But I didn't say it. There was no way I could stop their search. I winced to think how they would rummage through my possessions and rip apart

Professor Weaver's house. I had heard of police breaking down walls to look for drugs.

Desperately I wondered whether there was any way to dispose of my Lovedreamer sexy lingerie, my Estée Lauder anti-wrinkle crème, and the condoms in my bedside table drawer before Davis' and Clapton's knowing eyes detected them.

"Will you excuse me?" I said. "There are a few things upstairs I'd like to tidy."

Agnew snorted. "Forget it."

"Ma'am, we've seen everything," Constable Clapton said. "Don't worry about it."

"We'll start in the basement," Sergeant Davis said.

"Fine," I answered. "Should I go with you?"

"You're welcome to observe, so long as you don't try to obstruct the search or conceal evidence. On the other hand, you might prefer to wait with Detective Agnew in the living room."

"I'd rather observe," I said.

I followed Davis and Clapton down the cellar stairs. Davis went first to the washer, where the laundered sheets were ready to be put into the dryer. He lifted the lid and looked inside.

"Bedsheets," I said, helpfully.

"Hm." His tone was thoughtful. What was he thinking? Bloodstains?

He lowered the lid and looked in the dryer. Empty.

While Davis was inspecting my laundry equipment, Clapton crawled on his hands and knees under the cellar stairs, where Professor Weaver's shop-vac had been sitting undisturbed for at least as long as I had lived in his house.

Clapton emerged, rear-end first, and stood up. "It's clean," he said, wiping strands of cobwebs from his face and hair.

"Clean?" For a moment I thought he must be nuts.

Clapton smiled. "Disturbed cobwebs are the first sign that something has been hidden. Your cobwebs are intact."

"Good to know," I said.

The two men poked around in the basement for half an hour. They peered into corners and around joists. With the tip of a screwdriver, Clapton tapped the air ducts and heat ducts. He would give the galvanized metal a tap, move along a couple of feet, then tap again. Each tap produced a hollow clang. No briefcase in there.

"Now we'll check the ground floor," Davis said.

I trotted up the stairs after them.

The ground floor took longer. Fewer cobwebs. The two officers opened cupboards, pulled out drawers, and ransacked closets. They peered into the oven. By the time they had finished under the kitchen sink, pulling out bottles and cans of oven cleaner, toilet cleaner, and drain clearer, they had unearthed enough poison to kill every resident of Inchbury Street. They also found a mummified mouse.

"You don't have to put that back," I said when Clapton started clearing up. I picked up the dead mouse, using a paper towel. No signs of violence to the corpse. The tiny rodent appeared to have died of natural causes. How had Socrates allowed that to happen?

Next came the living room, where the built-in bookshelves attracted special interest.

"There's no dust on these books," Davis' voice was filled with suspicion. "Or on the shelves."

"I shelved those books only a week ago," I said. "They haven't had time to get dusty."

"Hm," Davis said as he started to empty the bookcase on the left of the fireplace. "I'll do this side," he said to Clapton. "You do the other."

"Surely you can see that the shelves are only eight inches deep," I protested. "There's no room to hide a briefcase behind those books."

"You'd be surprised how many built-in bookcases have a concealed compartment behind. Or a safe."

"Not these bookcases."

But there was no stopping the search, and the ramparts of books started to rise. I wondered whether the officers planned to put them back. If they didn't, I would not be able to ask Michael to help – unless I wanted to explain to him why my books were once again in stacks on the living room floor.

When the shelves were cleared, the wall tapping began. Tap tap. Tap, tap tap. I found myself becoming interested. Secret chambers are the stuff of mystery. Peering around Davis' shoulder, I looked for signs of a hidden latch and was slightly disappointed not to see one.

"Clean," Davis said.

"Same here," Clapton responded from his side of the fireplace.

The officers reshelved my books, and they did it with proper care. That was a relief.

When the officers had finished with the downstairs, I let them go to the second storey without me. Davis and Clapton were as cool as anyone could wish. But the thought of watching Agnew leer at my sexy lingerie was too much.

"I'll wait down here with Detective Agnew," I told them.

"Fine," said Davis.

As Davis and Clapton walked up the stairs, Agnew took me by the elbow and guided me into the living room. The gesture made me feel as if I were already under police escort, if not arrest. I shrugged off his hand, and then immediately regretted the rebuff. Why make an enemy of Agnew, if he were not already an enemy?

"Would you like a cup of coffee?" I forced a smile.

"Sure. Why not?"

I hoped that he would not follow me into the kitchen, but he did. His eyes were on me every moment while I filled the pot with water and measured the coffee into the filter. Clearly he had no intention of letting me out of his sight until the search ended.

The first drops of coffee splashed into the carafe, and as the rich aroma filled my nostrils, I took a deep breath.

"What do you take in your coffee?"

"Just black, no sugar."

I glanced at him from the corner of my eye. He was leaning against the counter. Seeing him relax, I felt some of the tension run out of me. Maybe I could ask a couple of questions.

"Detective, why aren't you looking for other suspects? Why are you concentrating on me?"

He shot back with his own question. “Why did you lie when I questioned you?”

“I didn’t lie.”

“You were concealing something, and that amounts to a lie.”

“Why do you think that?”

I lifted two mugs from the shelf, filled them, and handed one to Agnew. Without speaking, we returned to the living room. He sat on an upright chair, while I sank onto the sofa. I watched his fingers – thick fingers, with neatly trimmed nails – holding the mug.

From my bedroom, directly overhead, came the thump of heavy footsteps. My skin prickled as I waited for snickers or guffaws. There were none.

After a while the footsteps moved elsewhere. Faintly, I heard the searchers walking about in the study and spare bedroom. Then the sound of their tread ceased. They must have gone up to the attic.

If they felt obliged to unpack and repack every one of the nineteen cartons that held Professor Weaver’s books, searching the attic would take a long time. There were also a couple of trunks to open if they cared enough to force the locks. I did not know what was in those trunks, nor had Professor Weaver left me the keys. But since both trunks were deep in dust in a part of the attic festooned with cobwebs, Davis and Clapton would likely leave them alone. At a glance it should be obvious that no one had been into either trunk for years.

I finished my coffee, rested my head on the sofa back, and let my eyes drift to the framed A. J. Casson print on the opposite wall. "Opeongo Lake." I had never visited Opeongo Lake, but I loved that picture. It showed still water, and a point of land with a fallen tree bleached by sun and wind. Yellow hills in the background. A grey and lowering sky. Whenever I looked at that landscape, I thought of the closing days of the summer when Guy Gordon and I had planted trees. What was Guy doing now? Working in a mill? Probably he was married, with children. A different life from mine.

I closed my eyes and saw him, a figure in a dream, standing in shallow water by the shore, with his pant legs rolled to the knee. He was bending over, looking at something in the water. Then he straightened, lifted his head, and looked at me. His dark eyes were young and full of life. Then the image faded and was gone.

With a jolt, I opened my eyes and saw Agnew staring at me.

"Uh, oh. I guess I dozed off," I said.

From the hall came the squeaking of footsteps descending the stairs.

As the two officers entered the living room, Davis said, "We're finished in the house. We found two briefcases. One is Dr. Gunn's, stamped with her initials. Nothing in it. The other is stuffed with Income Tax returns from somebody named Archibald Weaver. They cover the years 1977 to 2002."

"Archibald Weaver owns the house," I explained. "I'm looking after it for a few years while he's out of the country."

Agnew hauled himself to his feet. "Pinkus' briefcase has got to be somewhere." He cast a grim glance at me, then addressed Davis and Clapton again. "I'm going back to headquarters. When you're done with the rest, I'll see you there."

After Agnew left, the other two went outside to search the garage, the garden and my car. I carried on with the laundry. At one point I looked out the window. Davis and Clapton were pacing through the garden. If they were looking for signs of digging, it would not take them long. Apart from the slight disturbance of soil where I had yanked spent daffodils from the flowerbeds, they would find nothing.

An hour later, when the search was complete, Davis asked me to sign a paper affirming that the premises were in good order, with no damage done. Before signing, I walked through the house, opening drawers and closets. Everything was fine.

Watching the officers drive away in their van, I hoped that now the police would leave me alone. Fat chance. I had the feeling that Agnew wasn't the type to give up.

# Eleven

Standing beside my freshly made bed, I felt tired, lonely and afraid. It was six o'clock, and the day had been lost, in terms of any productive activity. I wanted Michael in my bed tonight. Sleeping in his arms, I would feel safe.

All it would take was a phone call. He was sure to say yes. But what if the police had put a tap on my phone? I wouldn't want Detective Agnew to hear me invite a man to spend the night.

I went downstairs and stuck a solo gourmet dinner into the microwave. Filet of sole stuffed with spinach risotto. Then I poured myself a glass of Chardonnay. What should I do now? Given that I was a suspect in a murder case, I had a choice to make. Either I could sit at home and wait for the Atherton police to complete their investigation, or I could do my own.

Sitting and waiting would be easier. If I'd had more confidence in the Atherton Police Department, that is what I would have done. But Detective Agnew, having decided that I had a motive for murder, did not appear interested in looking for other suspects. In self-defence, I needed to conduct my own investigation, and the place to begin was Toronto.

Because nowadays I couldn't afford a Toronto hotel, my mother would have to take me in. All she knew about my present lack of employment was that my two-year contract had come to an end. Mom did not know about Sebastian. Since I wasn't about to tell her, I'd have to put up with her usual questions about my love life. Oh, well. There's no free lunch.

As soon as I had finished my supper, I picked up the phone. Even if there were a bug on the line, a call to my mother would not be incriminating. After two rings, Mom answered.

"Hello, Mom," I said. "It's me."

"Deirdre?"

"That's right."

"Is something the matter?"

"Of course not." *Was she psychic?* "But I have a few things to do in Toronto and thought you might put me up for a few days."

No mention of our quarrel. I had not expected that there would be. Mom could be exasperating, but she never held a grudge.

"When were you thinking of coming?"

"Tomorrow."

"In time for dinner?" I heard the eagerness in her voice. Mom loved to cook, but not for herself alone.

"Absolutely."

As we talked, I noticed a dark, feline shape leap onto the windowsill. Socrates, home for supper before his evening prowl. While I was away, he could stay outdoors. He would prefer that to being locked in with a tray of kitty litter.

After saying good-bye to Mom, I dutifully called the police station, as Agnew had instructed me to do if I planned to leave town. No problem there. Agnew asked for my mother's name, address and telephone number.

After I had given that information, he asked, "How long will you be away?"

"For the weekend. Friday to Monday."

"Call me when you get back."

In the morning, I fetched a suitcase from the attic and packed the basics. A three-day trip requires little. I would take along *Don Quixote,* of course, and my Holt Renfrew suit, just in case the need arose to impress anybody.

When I had finished packing, I set out a large bowl of water and a three-day supply of kibble, in three saucers, on the back porch.

"You'll have to stay here to look after the house," I told Socrates when he showed up for breakfast.

By tomorrow, he would have eaten all the food, unless raccoons got to it first. Either way, it didn't matter. If Socrates were really hungry, he could catch a mouse. I pushed him outside and locked the back door.

After checking that all the windows were secured, I picked up my suitcase and stepped onto the front porch. It was eleven o'clock. By setting out now, I could beat the Toronto rush hour and be at my mother's house by mid-afternoon. I locked the front door.

Across the street, Harold and Alma sat in their Muskoka chairs. Alma was watching me. Harold appeared to be asleep, with his head slumped forward and his chin resting on his chest. I set down my suitcase outside the front door and crossed the street to speak to Alma. It's a good idea to let the neighbours know when you will be away.

"I'm going to Toronto for a couple of days to visit my mother," I said. "I'll be back by Monday evening. I'd appreciate it if you'd keep an eye on the house."

Alma reached across the small wooden table that stood between the chairs and tapped Harold on the arm.

"Dr. Gunn says she's going to Toronto to visit her mother."

Harold opened his eyes and raised his head.

"Toronto, eh?" He pushed his glasses up the bridge of his nose. "I wouldn't go to Toronto if you paid me. Too much crime."

Following this pronouncement, he closed his eyes and let his chin sink to his chest again.

Alma said, "We used to go to the Ex in Toronto every year when the children were young. Do they still have it?"

"The Canadian National Exhibition? Yes, it's still going on."

"I especially enjoyed the Food Pavilion. All those free samples. Will you be going there?"

I was about to explain that the CNE took place at the end of August, whereas this was still late June, when I saw Alma's eyes open wide. She was looking at something behind me.

"There's that student of yours. Is he going to Toronto with you?"

Turning around, I saw Sebastian coming along the sidewalk. His pace was slow, and his arms hung limply.

"Oh, shit," I said.

Sebastian turned up my front walk and mounted the porch steps. He glanced at the suitcase, rang the doorbell, then stepped back and looked at the suitcase again.

"Pardon my language," I said to Alma. "I'd better speak to him. I don't know what he's doing here."

"Sebastian!" I called as I hurried across the street.

He turned and faced me. This time he looked sober, although his eyes were threaded with red. And he needed a haircut.

"Sorry about the other day," he mumbled apologetically. "I shouldn't have visited you in such a state, but I needed to talk to you."

"You and I have nothing to say to each other."

"Oh, I don't blame you for giving up on me. Everybody else has."

I glared at him. He looked at his shoes. There were beads of perspiration on his upper lip. It was a hot humid day, the sort of day when one's clothes stick heavily to one's skin.

"I'll get you a glass of water," I said. "You look wilted."

I unlocked the front door and went inside. Sebastian remained standing until I returned.

"Thank you," he said meekly when I handed him the glass.

We both sat down on the swing. He sipped at the water.

"My allowance has been cut in half because I failed my year."

"Well, you knew that might happen. It's time you grew up."

"Deirdre, I can't live on fifteen thousand a year."

"Fifteen thousand dollars?"

"Pounds."

"Plenty of people live on less." Christ, I thought, that's about thirty thousand Canadian dollars. Right now, I'd be happy with that income. If Sebastian expected sympathy, he'd come to the wrong place.

"I had to give up my apartment. I'm living at the Atherton Arms. You don't know how squalid –"

"Actually, I do!"

"Really?" His eyebrows lifted, inviting me to explain. But I didn't. My mind was racing ahead. I saw how Sebastian might for the first time be of some practical use to me.

"Go on," I said. "I didn't mean to interrupt."

He sighed. "My only hope is to write a supplemental examination in August. If I can pass even one course, I think my father will relent – partly relent, at least. I thought I might try English 201, since I didn't fail it quite as badly as the others. And I know you could help me."

"I could." A long pause. "But you would have to do something for me."

He smiled. "Anything."

I moved further away, crowding the wicker armrest at the other end of the swing.

"Recently," I said, "there was a murder at the Atherton Arms."

He nodded. "On Friday, two days before I moved in."

"The victim was somebody I knew."

"Did you?" His eyebrows shot up. "From what I heard about him, I wouldn't have thought him the sort of chap you'd likely know."

"It was a long time ago."

"Was he your lover?"

"Never. Not even my friend. I knew him when I was a student. He made contact with me about a week ago, the police learned about it, and now they are interested in me."

"Interested? In you? You can't mean ... ?" The look on his face was partly puzzlement and partly shock.

"As they say in your country, 'I'm helping the police with their investigation.'"

"That's appalling." He took a sharp breath. "But, why?"

"It's one of those cases of being in the wrong place at the wrong time. I happened to visit Pinkus' room shortly before he was found dead. Let's not go into that. It had nothing to do with sex. But while the police are scrambling about trying to uncover a motive for me to be the killer, I don't think they're making enough effort to find out who really did it. And that's where you can help me."

"Me? I'm not a private investigator."

"No. But you live at the Atherton Arms." I took a deep breath. "Sebastian, I'll make a bargain with you. I want you to find out everything you can about the crime scene. Talk to the maids. Make friends with the desk clerk and pick his brains. If there are any long-term guests, find out who saw what. Ask about possible rumours. Somebody may have an idea, even a hunch, who killed Pinkus. In return, I'll tutor you for the supplemental exam. Two hours every day. I guarantee a B Grade." I hesitated. "Providing you read the books."

Sebastian blinked. "When can we begin?"

"Tuesday morning, ten o'clock. I'm just leaving for Toronto. I'll be back Monday evening. That will give you a few days both to investigate and to start reading. I'll expect you to have finished Chaucer's Prologue to *The Canterbury Tales* before I return."

"All of it?"

"Every word. And now I must be off."

"Righto," he said, but without much enthusiasm.

Raising his right hand in a floppy salute, Sebastian left. As I watched him trudge toward the bus stop, I hoped that, for once, he might actually do something.

I carried the empty water glass into the house. After setting it on the kitchen counter, I thought about phoning Michael. New relationships require careful handling. I should not disappear for three days without mentioning that I would be away. There was a wall phone in the kitchen. I picked up the receiver, dialed the first three digits, and then stopped. And it wasn't just because there might be a bug on my phone.

If I said I was going to Toronto, Michael might ask why, and I didn't want to tell him. I still clung to the possibility that he need never know I was under investigation. Hanging up the receiver, I walked over to the window and looked outside. There was Socrates, crouched over his second saucer of kibble (the first already empty). He licked the saucer clean while I was making up my mind.

Then I went back to the telephone. It was noon already, lunch hour. If I phoned Michael now, there was a good chance I'd get Call Answering and wouldn't actually have to talk to him. No questions and no lies. Better that way. I picked up the receiver and this time dialed the entire number.

The phone rang once, twice, thrice, four times. "Hello. You have reached Michael Burton's voice mail. At the tone ..."

I was lucky.

"Hi, Michael," I said. "This is Deirdre Gunn. I'm going to Toronto for a few days to visit my mother. Back Monday night, in case you're looking for me – which I hope you are. Ha, ha!"

Shit! How did that stupid laugh slip out? That inadvertent "Ha, ha!" ruined the whole effect, made me sound like an idiot. If I cringed, how would Michael react? There was no way to erase it. I slammed the receiver into its cradle. Whenever I'm trying to act cool, why do I always spoil it with something spectacularly dumb? My poise rating sank ninety per cent.

Leaving the house, I locked the front door and, with a wave to Alma, carried my suitcase to the car. When visiting Toronto, I normally take the train. But this time, while carrying out my investigation, getting around would be easier if I had wheels.

I did not know where my investigation into George's death would lead me. But I had one further quest, a personal one that I had put off for a long time.

There are too many separate compartments in my life, I told myself as I drove onto the 401. Someday I'd have to get my whole act together: personal life, professional life, and financial affairs. Other people seem to manage it, and most of them don't have PhD's.

Setting the cruise control at 115 kilometres per hour – as fast as my ten-year-old BMW could go without starting to shudder, I left the window beside me open. The air conditioning had expired, and I couldn't spare the three hundred and fifty dollars it would cost to fix it.

First thing I'd do with the income from my scholarly edition of *Cardenio* was buy a new BMW. With air conditioning that worked. And a ten-speaker sound system. And a Panorama Sunroof. My new car would be silvery grey, with red leather seats. No. I look awful in red. Dark green would be better. Or black, if dark green wasn't available in leather.

After buying the car, I might splurge on travel. Italy, of course. And Australia. I'd never been to Australia. I could see myself slipping into an orchestra seat in the Melbourne Opera House, wearing my new Valentino suit – a step up from Holt Renfrew. On the way back to Canada, I might stop off in Shanghai for a little shopping.

As for my needs as a scholar, my critical edition of *Cardenio* would furnish the financial resources to crisscross the Atlantic as free as an albatross. (Whoops! Bad image.) London, Oxford, Cambridge – all academic doors would be open to me.

The kilometres clicked by, punctuated by turn-offs to towns I had never visited. What did people do in places where there was no university? Presqu'ile. Welcome. Bond Head. I imagined turning off the freeway, disappearing into some quiet village in the hills of Northumberland County, never to be seen again. There was something to be said for that too. Simplicity. Serenity. Maybe I could find a place like Brigadoon: here today, gone for the next hundred years.

Now Oshawa was behind me, and almost immediately, during the height of rush hour, I reached the Toronto gridlock.

But it wasn't too bad. Most of the Friday traffic was fleeing the city, not heading into it. By the time I drove into the driveway of the Gunn family home, it was suppertime.

My mother had left the kitchen window open. Even before leaving my car, I smelled fresh pie, the fragrance of cinnamon and apples wafting through the warm air. I sat for a moment, simply breathing. Mom led a cooking life. Food was her language, the medium through which she had always expressed her love for her family: Dad, now in a nursing home; Sheila, dead thirty years; and me on those rare occasions I returned home. Where another woman might have turned to Prozac, she baked a pie, gaining strength and comfort from the actions of peeling apples, cutting lard into flour, rolling out crust.

"Your banner over me is food," Dad had once said to her at the dinner table.

"You mean love," I had said, startled that he knew The Song of Solomon, even to misquote it.

"In this house, it's the same thing," he had answered.

Sitting in the driveway, smelling that apple pie, I recognized appeasement. Mom and I had had a rift, not only over the money she refused to lend me but also over the way I lived my life. Now I would eat her pie – humble pie – and be reconciled.

# Twelve

That evening, Mom and I were both on our best behaviour. She did not once mention her friends' grandchildren. I praised the poached salmon and braised asparagus she had prepared for my dinner and ate two slices of apple pie. Together we washed the dishes: she washed, I dried. In the cool of the evening we went outside, where she showed me the climbing rosebush she had planted against the back fence. It was a multi-flora, with cascades of yellow blossoms. The scents of roses and honeysuckle filled the air. When darkness fell, we went inside.

My mother lived alone in the house where she had spent fifty years of married life. It was a two-storey redbrick house, built in the 1930s. There were three bedrooms: my parents' bedroom, mine, and the one that had been Sheila's.

From as far back as I could remember, the matrimonial bedroom had not changed. Before I could properly read, I knew that the letters on the framed plaque above my parents' double bed spelled out: "God Bless this Home." My bedroom, too, had remained frozen in time ever since, at age seventeen, in a display of newly acquired sophistication, I had replaced my Elvis posters with Miro prints. Only my sister Sheila's bedroom had changed, having morphed into a sewing room when Mom's need for space to accommodate a cutting table banished Sheila's bed to the attic.

If the skirt that I wanted to wear the next day had not been crushed in my suitcase, I probably would not have entered the sewing room that evening. But the sewing room was where the ironing board was kept. Before going to bed, I decided that I should press my skirt.

Probably I was tired from the long drive, but for a split second when I switched on the light, I seemed to see pink-and-white-striped wallpaper, a single bed piled with stuffed animals, and a full-length mirror. The illusion was gone in an instant. Before me stood Mom's cutting table, her sewing machine, and the ironing board. Yet that swift impression carried me back to the evening more than thirty years ago when I had sat on Sheila's bed and watched her get ready for the prom. I was eight and she was sixteen. She wore pink lipstick and a brassiere and went to high school.

I remembered how she had stood in front of the mirror, tilting her head toward one shoulder, then the other, studying the sparkle of her earrings, which were like the prisms of the chandelier over our dining-room table, in miniature of course.

Sheila's hair was black, and her cheeks were pink, and her prom dress was pink. When she moved, it seemed to float about her. To me, she had looked like a princess.

Two Sheilas live in my memory: the blue-jeaned, pony-tailed girl of every day, and the radiant princess who waved good-bye. The boy who picked her up in his car was named Tommy. Thomas, my father called him. He was thin and taller than my father – which made him very tall, indeed.

Sheila carried a little evening bag embroidered with pearls. Later, my mother gave it to me to remember Sheila by. It's still in the top dresser drawer in my old bedroom.

The next morning my father woke me early to tell me that Sheila had gone away to heaven "to save a place for us." I imagined Sheila and her date in his car, soaring past the moon and the stars on their way to Paradise. Tommy also died in the crash that took Sheila's life. My parents never talked about him. Looking back on it, I suspect that he had been drinking. Probably all the kids had been drinking. But I never asked.

When I began my search for possible murder suspects, I had no clearer purpose than to offer the police a few options, to suggest other candidates besides myself. The sooner the police stopped pestering me, the sooner I could get on with *Cardenio*.

I wanted to learn who had been angry enough to want to kill George Pinkus. You cannot be a homosexual pedophile, I reasoned, without making quite a few people hate you.

Of course it was possible that George's death had no connection to his pedophilia. His career – if one could call it that – might have earned him enemies. How many people had he cheated? How often had he tried to peddle stolen property?

A personal vendetta was another possibility. I could not recall George having friends or enemies while at university. But since he had not been part of my circle, my ignorance meant little. Among the few acquaintances that George and I had in common, the poet Ken Hains was the one most likely to know something about George's private life. The three of us had been classmates. Ken had shared an apartment with George in second year.

Ken and I were still in touch. On visits to Toronto, I frequently dropped in at Ken's Den, his second-hand bookstore. I liked both Ken and his poetry, which appeared regularly in literary journals. I had visited Toronto to hear him read at the Art Bar. Every few years he brought out a chapbook, and I always purchased a copy.

Ken lived in an apartment above the bookstore, which was located in a narrow, two-storey brick building that he had bought with an inheritance in the days before Queen Street became trendy. The bookstore brought in just enough to support him and his poetry habit.

My inquiries began with Ken.

I left my car in a parking lot a couple of blocks from Ken's Den. Walking slowly, thinking about what I was going to say, I stopped now and then to look into shop windows. The Great Wall Import Store had in its display a ceramic elephant the size of a pot-bellied pig, hand-painted with blue birds, green leaves, and pink peonies. I wondered how many people would want a ceramic elephant in their living room.

As I approached the bookstore, I saw Ken through the window, sitting behind the counter reading a book. A bell above the door jangled when I entered.

"Deirdre!" Ken jumped up. "I didn't know you were in town." He came around the counter and gave me a kiss on each cheek. "You're looking good, as usual."

"You too," I said tactfully.

Ken was of middle height, with a prominent Adam's apple, narrow shoulders and jutting hipbones that the tightness of his jeans emphasized. Black jeans and a black turtleneck were his uniform. He had a beak-like nose and dark blond hair, which he wore pulled back in a ponytail fastened with a leather thong.

"This calls for a drink," he said.

Ken took the "Open" sign from its hook on the door and replaced it with one that stated, "Back in One Hour." He always did this when I dropped in. Since I had never seen a customer in the store, I didn't suppose that it made much difference to the amount of business he did.

To reach Ken's apartment we climbed a flight of stairs at the rear of the shop. The steps had been painted grey, but the centre part of the treads had been worn down to bare wood for as long as I had been visiting Ken.

Sometimes a woman drifted through Ken's life. One had stayed a couple of years, moving on when forced to admit that she would always play second fiddle to his poetry. The apartment always looked brighter and cleaner during these semi-marital relationships. But today, the thickness of dust on the furniture and the quantity of newspapers strewn over the floor were evidence that Ken's most recent lady had departed some time ago.

Ken lifted a sheaf of loose papers that looked like poetry manuscripts from the seat of a chair, set them on a side table, and pushed the chair toward me. He perched on one arm of the sofa. No one could have sat on the seat cushions, because they were piled high with old books.

"Stuff I just got in," he said, waving his hand at them. "Maybe you'd like to have a look?"

"Not this time. What I've come for is information."

"What about?"

I plunged right in. "George Pinkus. I was hoping you could tell me what he'd been up to lately. You know he's been murdered?"

Ken sucked in his breath. "I read about that. It happened in Atherton, didn't it? That's your neck of the woods."

"Yes. And that's the problem. The police found my name in his address book."

"Really? I didn't know that you and George kept in touch."

"We didn't. I was astonished when he showed up in Atherton about ten days ago. He contacted me, and we saw each other a few times. Unfortunately, I dropped into his hotel room shortly before he was murdered. The police are dreaming up reasons why I might have wanted to kill him. Before they get any further, I thought I'd look for leads to other people who might have had a motive."

"Not me, I hope?"

I laughed. "I didn't have you in mind. Besides, I don't imagine you've been to Atherton lately."

"Never, in fact." He stood up. "Beer okay?"

Without waiting for an answer, he disappeared into the kitchen and returned with two bottles of lager, no glasses. He handed one to me and perched again on the arm of the sofa.

"George had enemies," he said. "All those boys he abused, plus their parents. People he cheated, one way or another. There must have been quite a few who hated him." Ken tilted the bottle and took a gulp of beer. "George and I didn't part on friendly terms. For one year we shared an apartment, as you know. When the rent came due, he never seemed to have any money. After the university expelled him for plagiarism, he took off, owing me two hundred bucks. At the time, it was a fair bit of cash." Ken took another swig. "If I'd run into him twenty years ago, I would have felt like killing him myself."

"Did you never see him again?"

"Oh, I saw him again. But not for about ten years. By then I'd stopped feeling bitter, and the money didn't matter so much. My grandfather had left me a nice legacy, enough to survive so long as I was careful. Ken's Den had been open for only a couple of weeks when George walked in with a carton of books he said he had inherited. I didn't totally believe that, knowing George. More likely he'd swindled some poor widow. There were a couple of rare first editions among the books he showed me, so I bought the lot. Maybe I should have asked questions."

"How did he seem?"

"Full of plans. He said he was interested in getting into the rare book business, and what did I think?"

"What did you tell him?"

"That there wasn't any money in it. I said he'd better forget it, unless he cherished books. You know, bibliophiles are like poets – a bit mad. George struck me as being greedy, but on a small scale. A little fish in a little pond."

I set my beer, untouched, on the coffee table between a stack of *National Geographic* magazines and a Bruegel art book that had a picture of soldiers filleting peasants on the front cover.

"You saw him just that once?" I asked.

"No. He brought in more books from time to time, both before and after the years he spent in prison. The last time was about six weeks ago. He showed me a battered old manuscript play called *Cardenio.*"

"What!"

"He said it was Shakespeare's lost play, and I could have it for two hundred grand. I told him that if it was authentic and he had come by it honestly, he'd be better off shopping it to the Folger Institute in Washington. George wasn't pleased to hear me say that – told me I was passing up a chance to make a fortune. He went off in a huff, and I never saw him again."

The dirty rat! All that talk about me being the chosen one to present *Cardenio* to the world. As far as I knew, George could have been peddling that manuscript all over North America.

"Deirdre? Something wrong?"

"Uh, no. Do you suppose I could have a glass for this beer?"

"Sure." He brought a glass from the kitchen. It was streaky with a lipstick smear on the rim. I wished I hadn't asked.

As I poured my beer, I said, "Did George ever talk about prison?"

"Not to me."

"What about his private life?"

"We never discussed it. I know he was married for a while, but it came out at the trial that the marriage was camouflage. You know, a cover so people wouldn't suspect him of liking boys. His wife's name was Sarah. She divorced him around the time he went to prison."

"I don't suppose she uses the name Pinkus?"

"She never did, even while they were married. Her last name is Morrison. She plays the organ at Redeemer United Church."

"Thanks. I'll look her up."

"She might give you some names."

As soon as I'd finished my beer, I said I had to be leaving.

"I'll phone you if I learn anything more about George," he said. "Or send you an e-mail."

"You may not have my new address. I had to change it. Too much spam."

"Better give me your new one, then. In case I don't already have it."

He set down his empty bottle between Bruegel and the *National Geographics*. "There must be a piece of paper somewhere around here." His eyes roamed over the general disorder, finally settling on the manuscript of a poem. "This will do." He picked it up. "Now for a pencil."

"Here's a pen," I said, spotting one half hidden by newspapers on the floor. It was a red ballpoint. As I pulled it from under the newspaper, I noticed that it was one of those promotional pens that advertise a business: 'Bide Your Time Budget Motel/Atherton, Ontario.'

It was on the tip of my tongue to ask where he had got the pen. But I stopped myself and simply handed it to him.

Ken did not notice my moment of hesitation. I'm sure of that. After jotting down my e-mail address, he followed me down the stairs to the shop. Then he hung the "Open" sign back on the door.

*The pen means nothing,* I told myself as I walked to my car. I had a ballpoint at home that advertised a collision repair shop in Dundas. I've never been to Dundas. Ken said that he had never been to Atherton; I wanted to believe him.

# Thirteen

What sort of woman would marry George Pinkus?

The church secretary directed me to Sarah Morrison's home. It was a row house two blocks from the church, on a narrow street with a "No Parking Without Permit" sign on every lamppost. For twenty minutes I drove around the neighbourhood before finding a place to leave my car. By the time I had walked four blocks from my parking spot to Sarah Morrison's front door, I felt sticky with perspiration.

The house was narrow, twenty feet wide at most, two storeys high, and identical to the other four houses in the row. The door was painted blue. A white, gauzy curtain, the kind that has a rod at both top and bottom to hold it taut, covered the door window. There was no porch, but only a single step to the threshold.

Inside the house, someone was playing the piano. Beethoven's *Für Elise.* Long ago I had struggled with that piece for a Royal Conservatory of Music examination. I waited until the end before ringing the bell.

Through the curtain I saw a woman's shape approaching. The door opened. Wary blue eyes peered at me through thick glasses.

"Sarah Morrison?" I asked.

She nodded.

"My name is Deirdre Gunn."

"Yes?"

" I need to talk to you about George Pinkus. About his death."

"I don't know anything about it." I think she was waiting for me to flash a badge. After half a minute she said, "How does it concern you?"

"The police have been questioning me. And since I didn't kill George, I'd like to know who did."

"Shouldn't you leave that to the police?"

"Not when their efforts appear to be entirely focussed on me."

"That's no concern of mine."

A sharp edge had entered her voice. The look in her eye said, *Go away.* Any second now, she would close the door in my face. I saw it coming. Like a door-to-door salesman in an old comedy, I pressed my foot against the jamb.

When she slammed the door, I yelped, "You didn't need to break my foot!"

Her expression changed. Now anxiety filled her eyes and furrowed her brow.

"I'm so sorry!" She opened the door enough to free my foot. "Do you think it is broken?"

"Possibly."

A sigh. "You'd better come in."

I hopped inside. Facing me was a small woman, five-foot-nothing, maybe one hundred pounds. The top of her head was barely up to my chin. Her skin was pallid, and her hair mouse-coloured. She wore a white blouse, a limp cardigan, and a skirt of no particular style. Everything about her was meagre. Though probably about my age, she looked old.

I took a step, winced more than was necessary.

"You'd better sit down," she said, and gestured for me to go ahead of her into the front room. I sat down on a green-and-grey striped upholstered chair. The room was small, and crammed with bric-a-brac that looked a hundred years old. Inherited, I supposed. An upright piano with yellowed keys dominated the space.

My instep throbbed. Since I was wearing sandals, the red mark where the edge of the door had struck was clearly visible. My foot was starting to swell.

"I'm so sorry," she said again, and actually wrung her hands.

This woman obviously carried a huge burden of guilt. I suppressed the urge to tell her that the injury was as much my fault as hers.

"Would you like a cup of tea?" she asked.

"I'd love one."

While she put on the kettle, I thought how lucky I had been to get my foot crushed in her door.

She brought the tea things on a silver tray: china pot with matching sugar bowl and pitcher, porcelain cups and saucers, a plate of shortbreads. After setting the tray on a low table, she poured the tea.

"The police came to see me too," she said. "They asked about people George knew. Since I'd never heard him mention your name, you were not among them." She tilted her head politely. "Milk and sugar?"

"Neither, thanks."

She handed me a cup.

I sipped delicately. "I knew George when we both were undergraduates at King's College. Afterwards, we lost touch. I didn't realize that he had married."

"Our marriage lasted only two years. It was a terrible mistake."

"These things happen." I ventured a tone of intimacy. "I've never been married. As the years pass, I suspect that I never shall be."

Our eyes met. "When I met George," she said, "I was in my mid-thirties. Though you may find this difficult to believe, I'd never had ..." She glanced away. "A close relationship with a man."

This did not surprise me. There are people who spend their entire lives invisible to the opposite sex.

She continued, "It was flattering to be courted. Oh, I had no illusions about George. Whenever he invited me out for a meal, he always seemed to have forgotten his wallet. Sometimes he would borrow ten or twenty dollars, and I could never bring myself to ask for it back."

She pushed the cookies toward me. "Do have one."

While I nibbled the shortbread, she explained, "I suspect he married me for my house. It may be small, but I own it free of any mortgage. George never took me to where he lived. I knew the address. Probably he rented a room or a basement apartment." Her voice was so low that I had to lean forward to hear every word. "I knew that George was self-employed. He tutored boys with learning difficulties, going to their homes to give lessons. After we married, the boys started coming here. George said it was more dignified than for him to traipse all over town.

"My job was to serve tea and cookies, and then leave. I don't mean leave the room. I mean leave the house. At the time this made sense, because my home is very small, as you see."

"He made you leave the house? And you noticed nothing wrong?"

"If I had been suspicious, I might have." Her pale cheeks flushed. "George had me completely fooled. He said it would be a distraction to have me there. Even if I stayed in the bedroom, he'd be constantly worrying I'd make some sort of noise that would disrupt concentration. So I'd walk over to the church and practice the organ. I didn't mind."

"You must be bitter."

"Bitter? Perhaps. But ashamed is the word that comes first to mind. It was humiliating to have been taken in by such a man. There was a time when I thought I would never survive the disgrace." Her eyes hardened. "Ms. Gunn, I shed no tears for George. Whoever killed him did the world a favour. I hope the police never catch him."

"Or her?"

"Or her. The mothers of those boys hated George as much as the fathers did."

"Can you give me names?"

"Oh, no. I don't want to do that."

"Would you rather the wrong person went to prison?"

Her eyes blinked behind the thick lenses. "That would be a terrible injustice." Her hand holding the teacup shook visibly. Slowly she lowered it to the table. "To tell the truth,

I didn't know the boys' surnames, or even the given names of most of them. There were so many." A minute slipped by while she seemed to forget about me. "The parents blame me, some of them. They think I helped to set a trap for their sons." Her lower lip trembled. "Is your foot feeling better?"

I recognized the hint. "It's going to be fine."

Gulping the rest of my tea, I set down the cup. "Is there truly nothing you can tell me? Is there no one else I can ask?"

Shaking her head, she got to her feet, and I limped after her into the hall.

I was just leaving, my uninjured foot poised to step onto her front stoop, when she said, "Rosemary Cranshaw might talk to you. Her son was one of the victims. He took his own life."

"Where does she live?"

"In Rosedale. Wait a second and I'll write down the address."

When she returned with a slip of paper, I glanced at it and thrust it into my handbag.

"Thank you." I laid my hand on her forearm. "It wasn't your fault. George used you just as he used everybody."

"Good-bye," she said as I left. "I'm sorry about your foot."

I kept up the limp for appearance's sake till the end of the block.

It was five o'clock, too late to drive across town to Rosedale. I'd save Mrs. Cranshaw for tomorrow morning. This evening I would spend with my mother.

Navigating the currents of rush-hour traffic along Bloor Street, I made my way back home. Mom, wearing a green apron in a pattern sprigged with white flowers, stood at her kitchen counter with a large knife in her hand, expertly slicing carrots on a wooden cutting board.

"Need any help?" I asked.

"No." She looked up and smiled. "But you can keep me company."

I grabbed a chair and sat down to watch as she dealt methodically with carrots, turnips, potatoes and onions. Then she turned her attention to the shoulder of lamb that sat oozing blood on a platter. My mother made stew the way her mother had done fifty years ago in Ireland.

"This is for tomorrow," she said. "With stew, I like to rest it for a day. Tonight we'll just have a salad and cold cuts, if that's all right with you. And then we'll visit your dad. You know how he loves to see you."

"At Christmas, he didn't recognize me."

"Don't say that, Deirdre." Her hand holding the knife stopped moving. "You don't know what goes on inside his head."

Her mouth twisted and her eyes looked damp. Already I felt ashamed. How could I be sure that Dad had not recognized me? Because he had not said my name? Names are labels. Even though my label had been lost, he might still know who I was, and love me.

"Sorry," I said. "Let me make the salad, anyway."

"Thank you," she said stiffly.

I found lettuce, a red onion, mushrooms and a sweet yellow pepper in the crisper. I was washing the lettuce when Mom spoke up. "Deirdre, you'll find some sliced ham in the refrigerator. We can have that with the salad. For dessert, there's a bit of apple pie from last night."

After supper, Mom changed from slacks into a dress – dark blue with white polka dots – pantyhose and pumps. It was one of those humid evenings when the air feels sticky. I didn't know how she could stand the feel of nylon encasing her legs.

"Isn't it too hot for pantyhose?" I asked her as we were about to leave the house. "It isn't as if Dad will notice what you're wearing."

"That's not the point." She said no more until we were in the car – my car. My mother had never learned to drive. For two years she had visited my father every day, taking the subway and a bus each way. "Do you remember," she said as I backed out of the driveway, "when you were little, I always combed my hair and put on lipstick before your father arrived home from work?"

I didn't remember, but waited for her to go on.

"I owed it to him," she continued, "to be the same person he had married. And I owe it to him now."

I said nothing. So my mother was dressing up to impress the man she had fallen in love with more than fifty years ago. How could I criticize that? In the face of such commitment, I felt ashamed … and slightly envious too.

The nursing home was called Innisfree Gardens. Mom had placed Dad there because she liked the name. From the stiff way she walked from the parking lot, you would think she had a steel rod for a spine, and when we rang the buzzer at the front door, her face changed as if she dropped a veil to cover her feelings.

At the reception desk, a plump woman with salt-and-pepper hair nodded as we passed by.

"She's a volunteer," Mom whispered. "She spends ten hours a week working here. Her mother is a resident. She thinks her mother gets better care because she's around to keep an eye on things."

We paused at the first set of glass doors while Mom punched numbers on a keypad. The doors opened for us, closing automatically after we had passed through. From waist-height up to the ceiling, the corridor wall on our right was glass. While Mom marched resolutely, eyes front like a soldier into battle, I surveyed the residents in their lounge on the other side of the glass. Three old women and an old man sat on upholstered chairs. The man's chin rested on his chest. The women sat impassively, their eyes glazed. A fitted bookcase at one end of the lounge held a set of *Reader's Digest* volumes on one shelf. The five other shelves were empty.

More buttons to push, more doors to open, and we entered the second circle of hell. Five wheelchairs parked in a row faced a TV screen tuned to CNN. No one was watching. One woman, secured in her wheelchair by straps around her waist and across her chest, howled continuously. Nobody appeared to notice, neither the other residents nor the staff member who walked through.

Dad's area came next, after another pad of buttons. The room we entered smelled of urine and Lysol. A large oak table, like a boardroom table, took up much of the space.

My father was alone, his head flung back and his eyes closed. He was wearing the dark green cardigan that Mom had knitted him ten years ago, and baggy sweatpants that looked three sizes too large. His wheelchair had been pushed up to the table for some reason, though the entire surface was empty.

I pulled Dad's wheelchair away from the table and turned it to face a pair of empty chairs that stood along the wall. Mom and I sat down. Dad's head now flopped forward. His forearms rested on the arms of the wheelchair, hands drooping over the ends. I noticed how waxy and white his fingers looked, his nails trimmed short and very clean. His one foot was on the footrest, the other dangled to the floor. He moaned in his sleep.

"Bernard," Mom said loudly. "Look who I brought to see you."

His eyes opened.

"Sheila?" He struggled to rise, but could not because of the straps that restrained him.

Mom protested, "Bernie, this isn't Sheila. It's Deirdre."

He gazed at me blankly. "Do I know you?"

I recoiled, unable to speak.

"Take his hands," Mom said, her voice urgent. "Help him to remember." Her voice faltered. "Help him ..."

A hot, sore lump seemed to fill my throat, and I fought back tears as I leaned toward him. I grasped his hands. "I'm your other daughter," I said. "The one with red hair."

His eyes brightened. He was alert, listening.

"I'm Sheila's little sister, the brat who got in trouble at school for arguing with the teachers."

A broad smile spread across his face. He said nothing, but I felt his fingers squeezing mine. I squeezed back. He squeezed harder. And his eyes glowed with feeling as they looked into mine.

# Fourteen

Mrs. Cranshaw lived on the edge of Rosedale, in the sort of house I would choose to live in if I had three million to spend on a home. It was an ivy-covered brick house set far back from the street. The leaves of locust trees traced delicate shadows on half an acre of green lawn. A long, curving drive swept between massive rhododendron bushes on its way to the front door. The style of the house was Victorian, with pillars at the entrance and a conservatory jutting from one side. As I parked my car, I was glad that I had decided to wear the Holt Renfrew suit – my substitute for a calling card.

A maid wearing a stiffly starched black dress with a white cap and apron answered the door. Except on stage or screen, I had never before seen anyone in a get-up like that. Middle-aged and of medium height and build, she wore her brown hair in a bun at the nape of her neck. Her forehead was broad, her eyes small, and her mouth firm. With her features so composed that her lack of expression must have been deliberate, she appeared to be the perfect servant, the loyal retainer who could be counted on to know her employers' standards and to anticipate their wishes. When I gave my name, the maid admitted me to the entrance hall and said she would inform Mrs. Cranshaw that she had a visitor. Once again, I felt grateful to Holt Renfrew.

Mrs. Cranshaw, when she arrived, was a surprise. Her face was gaunt, her cheekbones craggy, and her salt-and-pepper hair looked as if it had been hacked rather than cut. Dark circles around her eyes spoke of grief and sleepless nights. She wore a decidedly old plaid shirt and stained brown slacks. In every possible way her appearance differed from my image of a Rosedale matron.

"Ms. Gunn?" She looked at me suspiciously with dark, piercing eyes. "Have we met?"

I shook my head. "I don't believe so."

I had rehearsed in my mind exactly how I would approach Mrs. Cranshaw. I would be sympathetic, apologize for speaking of something that would bring back the pain of her loss, and then with utmost tact introduce the murder. But all my strategy flew out the window at the sight of her haggard face.

"I seldom have visitors," she said in a tone suggesting that this was deliberate. "Ellen uses her judgment about whom to admit."

"Forgive me this intrusion. But it won't take long. I've come to ask your help."

"What help could I give you?"

"It's about George Pinkus. You've read … I'm sure you know … what happened to him?"

Her face turned pale.

"Yes," she said. "It's been much in the news."

"His former wife, Sarah Morrison, said that you might have information about the way his actions affected people's lives." I paused, knowing that I had no right to be here.

Mrs. Cranshaw's dark eyes grew huge with alarm. "Are you a journalist? If you're from the media, I can't talk to you."

"No. I teach at Melrose University in Atherton." (A small lie.) "And I knew George Pinkus many years ago."

"As a friend?"

"Never as a friend. I knew what he was like, but he still found a way to prey on me. The truth is, the police suspect me of killing him. If you don't wish to talk to me, I understand. But I'm innocent, and have no desire to be convicted for a crime I did not commit."

As we looked into each other's eyes for a moment, I saw the change in her expression, the alarm replaced by elation. Her laughter was a deep-throated chuckle that made me shiver. "If it had been you who killed him, I'd shake your hand."

I didn't know how to answer, but I did not need to. Her hand darted forth suddenly and clutched mine.

"Come into the conservatory."

Her wiry fingers holding fast to mine, she led me from the front hall to the dining room and through a pair of open French doors into the conservatory. The earthy smell of peat moss and humus filled my nostrils. It felt like a rain forest in there, green and steamy. Staghorn ferns reached out their forked leaves from dripping nests of sphagnum moss. Epiphytes crouched in the crotches of a ceiling-high fig tree.

"I live here," she said, "with my plants. The rest of the house is Ellen's domain."

I could see that she meant it. On a small arborite table-top stood a breakfast tray that had not yet been cleared away. A narrow cot pressed against the wall opposite a bank of windows.

"Ralph left me, you know." Mrs. Cranshaw's fingers caressed the wax-like single petal of a peace lily, and then strayed to the green and crimson flower of a bird-of-paradise plant. I supposed that Ralph had been her husband.

She crossed the tiled floor to a small sink set in a stainless steel counter. On the counter stood half a dozen empty clay pots, a sprayer, a bottle of plant food, and a green plastic watering jug. She opened the bottle and, using a dropper, measured a dose before filling the jug with water.

"Sit down, if you like. You may watch while I feed my baby."

I settled in a cane chair.

Lifting a potted azalea with both hands, she set it on the counter while she poured water into its saucer. "Harry liked the azaleas best. Every winter this one was covered with flowers the colour of cotton candy." She returned the plant to its saucer.

"When Harry told us about Mr. Pinkus, Ralph went to the police. Harry didn't want him to. He was thirteen, and didn't want anyone to know what had happened. 'Everybody will think I'm gay,' is what he said. He threatened to run away from home if we reported the abuse. Ralph told Harry that nobody would divulge his name, because he was under age, you see. Harry was still unhappy about it, but Ralph went to the police anyway."

I said nothing. What could I say, knowing what came next?

Mrs. Cranshaw picked up the sprayer and spritzed the azalea. "This used to be Harry's job, from the time he was three years old. He liked to squirt water at the plants." She moved down the row, misting each in turn.

"When Ralph went to the police, Harry was terribly upset. But he seemed to be getting over it, until that social worker got hold of him. She told Harry that most people like Mr. Pinkus had themselves been sexually abused when they were young." Mrs. Cranshaw looked up from misting the plants. "What did that woman expect a thirteen-year-old boy to make of such information? He never passed it on to us. All we noticed was his silence. If Harry hadn't left a suicide note, we never would have known."

She picked up a pair of secateurs. "I blame that stupid, stupid woman. Harry's note said that he'd rather die than grow up to hurt children the way Mr. Pinkus hurt him. After Ralph and I lost Harry, our marriage fell apart."

I shifted in my seat, not knowing what to say.

"Harry had my dark eyes and my hair." She raised one hand to her salt-and-pepper thatch. "Black as a raven's wing." She laughed. "Ralph saw Harry every time he looked at me. Finally he moved out. We aren't divorced. He has an apartment on St. Clair. He says we may have to sell the house. Everything costs so much. And there are Ellen's wages too. Ralph knows I can't manage without her."

Mrs. Cranshaw held up the secateurs. "If I had Mr. Pinkus at my mercy, I'd do some deep pruning." She snapped the blades open and shut. "You know what parts

I'd cut off? I'll bet you do." She tittered. "Ralph said he'd take care of George Pinkus if he ever got his hands on him. But now he doesn't need to. That book is closed."

She nipped off the long, knobby, bare shoot of a hoya plant. "These are my children now. I hate to hurt them, but they do better for a little cutting back." She gave me a sideways glance. Her dark eyes glittered. "Do you suppose that plants feel pain?"

"No, I don't think they can." I stood up. Those secateurs made me nervous. "Thanks for talking with me. I have to get going now."

"It's a pity you couldn't meet Ralph," Mrs. Cranshaw laid the secateurs on the counter. "But he doesn't live here any more."

She crowded my elbow as we walked back through the dining room. When we reached the entrance hall, she grabbed my arm with a fierce grip and pushed her face close to mine. I could feel her breath.

"I'm the one who found Harry," she whispered hoarsely. "Did you know that? Did Ralph tell you that? Harry was in the basement. He'd hanged himself with a lamp cord. When I cut him down, he was still alive. Ellen called the ambulance."

I drew in my breath, tried to think of something to say. All that came out was, "Oh! No!" The "no" drawn out like a moan.

"They could have saved Harry. He'd still be alive. I could have looked after him." Her fingers felt like talons on my arm. "Ralph told me we had to let them pull the plug. The doctors said our boy would just be a vegetable." She laughed. "Ha! Ha! Ha! My son the turnip." Her fingers dropped from my arm, and she clapped them to her mouth. "Ha! Ha! Ha!"

I pushed off from her, shouting, "Ellen! Ellen! Come here!"

She was still laughing when Ellen appeared, running from the back part of the house, her face still impassive, as if this were nothing new. Ellen took Mrs. Cranshaw in her arms, rocking her gently.

I left with no farewell.

Time's a great healer, I thought as I drove away, but not when an abscess spreads its poison within a wound.

When I walked into the kitchen, my mother was standing at the counter spooning dark, creamy batter into a pair of cake pans.

"Mm! Chocolate!" I said, dipping my finger into the bowl.

Mom smiled. "Stop that! This is for dinner tonight."

As I licked my finger, I watched her scrape the bowl.

"A man phoned this morning asking for you," she said. "He told me his name was Andrew, or something like that."

"Agnew?"

"Yes, that was it. He wanted to know if you were staying with me. I asked if he wished to leave a number so you could call him. He said that was okay, and he'd see you when you got back."

"Fine."

"He had a nice voice. Quite deep. He sounded older than some of the men you've dated. A widower, maybe? You wouldn't want to get involved with a married man."

"I'm not involved with him. It's a professional matter."

From the way she sighed, I knew that my holiday from The Speech had ended.

"It's not that you couldn't have married, if you'd set your mind to it. You always had boyfriends. It's just that you scared them away by being too brainy. No man wants a wife who is smarter than him."

"Mother! I don't want to hear this."

"Oh, I don't mean to criticize you. Anyway, there's still time. Your own grandmother went on having a baby every year until she was forty-eight."

Mom put the filled cake pans into the oven.

I beat a retreat to my old bedroom. My mother had behaved so well for the past three days, but now she had cracked. I knew I would blow my stack if she started talking about all her friends who had ten grandchildren apiece. Better to stay in hiding for a couple of hours, with Cervantes for company.

*Don Quixote* was at hand, sitting on the same scuffed, maple desk that had been in this room since I went to high school. I sat down at the desk, checked my notes, and found my place in the book.

Cardenio, now accompanied by Don Quixote, Sancho Panza, a priest and a barber, is still wandering in the wild mountains of the Sierra Morena while cursing Luscinda and Don Fernando for their treachery. But in Chapter XXVIII a new character enters, restoring Cardenio's dreams.

Notes on Episode 3

- Enter: a shepherd boy, singing.
- Shepherd boy turns out to be Fernando's ex-sweetheart, Dorotea. She's in disguise, hiding in the mountains to conceal shame at losing her virginity.
- Dorotea explains how Don Fernando seduced her with holy vows promising marriage, before abandoning her to marry Luscinda.
- Cardenio is excited at this news, which apparently means that Fernando's marriage to Luscinda is void.
- Dorotea describes the events that followed the wedding. Hidden in Luscinda's clothing were a suicide note explaining she was already pledged to Cardenio, and a dagger. Fernando seized both. He read the note. Furious at such public humiliation, he tried to stab Luscinda with the dagger.
- Dorotea relates that Luscinda too has run away. Whereabouts unknown.
- Cardenio reveals his identity to Dorotea. Overjoyed that Fernando and Luscinda are not married after all, Cardenio declares that he will find Fernando and force him to keep his promise to Dorotea.

At last the end was in sight! One more episode should restore Luscinda to Cardenio and Fernando to Dorotea in holy matrimony – the usual all's-well-that-ends-well conclusion that Jacobean audiences loved.

Mom called from downstairs, "Dinner's ready."

I put *Don Quixote* and my notes into my suitcase. This was the last evening of my visit. Time to feast on Irish stew and chocolate cake. Time to make peace with Mom. That would not be difficult. On the whole, I considered, we had gotten along well during the weekend. Of course, Mom would never be able to understand me. But the failure was mutual, I supposed, as was the love between us.

My investigation had left me exhausted, and I was unsure how much I had accomplished. Was it enough to persuade the Atherton police to follow a different line of inquiry? I could only hope.

I had one piece of business still to attend to before returning to Atherton. It would be a search of a different sort.

# Fifteen

Sounds of a summer night. With the bedroom window open, I heard crickets chirping in the garden and, from two blocks south, traffic moving along Bloor Street. Above the steady murmur, horns honked and sirens wailed from time to time. I liked the night sounds of the city.

Although the sounds did not disturb me, I could not fall asleep. On visits to the house where I grew up, I seldom slept well. Too many memories tugged at my mind. In this same narrow bed, my fifteen-year-old self had fretted about boys, prom invitations, and what to wear to school the next day.

Did my daughter, when she was fifteen, fret about the same things? By giving her up, I had lost the opportunity to know her during those years of growing up. I never saw the changing stages of her progress from infancy through childhood and adolescence. Twenty-one years had passed since the one time I saw her scrunched-up red face and dark monkey eyes peeping above the hospital blanket. I had unwrapped her, inspected the stump of the umbilical cord that had so recently connected her to me. I had counted her fingers and toes, and then wrapped her up again.

"Don't bring her back," I told the nurse. "I can't keep her. I don't want to see her again."

The social worker from the Catholic Children's Aid Society, who showed up the next morning, told me that I had seven days to make up my mind.

"My mind's already made up," I told her.

I gave my daughter the name Pauline, my paternal grandmother's name, when a nurse said I had to call her something. A name was necessary for her birth certificate. Otherwise I would have left her nameless, hoping that the lack of a name would make her easier to forget. But they say you cannot forget that you have had a child.

I had given her up forever, or so I thought, not foreseeing that a decade later more liberal laws would allow the opening of adoption records. The birth mother had to apply. The child, now an adult, also had to apply. If a match were found, the two could meet.

In the language of crime investigation – a language I was learning fast – this provided opportunity. But what about motive? Maybe it was The Speech finally breaking down my defences – not that I had the slightest desire to procreate on the same scale as my maternal grandmother. The world would be buried in garbage, poisoned by pollution, if everyone reproduced at such a rate. But to tell Mom that she actually did have a grandchild, to bring that person to her home, lead her into my mother's kitchen. *Mom, here's somebody I want you to meet.* Just thinking about it brought tears to my eyes.

Any other motive, conscious or unconscious? Maybe the dearth of stable relationships in my life was prompting me, the cry of my heart for a blood relationship, unchangeable and irreversible, although unknown.

But was it a good idea? In literature, parent/child reunions had a bad record. Think Oedipus and Jocasta. Think Sorhab and Rustum. If that's the way things turn out, it would be smarter to forget the whole idea. Much smarter. But I did not need to decide tonight. Better wait and see how I felt in the morning.

Deciding not to decide let me off the hook. I fell asleep.

The next morning, still undecided, I hugged Mom good-bye. She watched from the doorway as I got into my car. Maybe she wondered why it took me so long to turn the ignition key. I waved and smiled as I backed out of the driveway, letting her know that there was no problem.

I still was not sure what I was going to do. But by the time I had reached Bloor Street and turned left towards Yonge instead of steering north to the 401, I realized that the die was cast.

All I had was an address, 38 Isabella Street, that I had looked up in the telephone directory. Toronto Catholic Children's Aid Society. Having given my child into their care, I would seek their help to find her again.

The traffic was slow. Bumper to bumper. Stop and start. Every lane full. The first light I came to turned yellow as I approached. I stopped, waiting for the green, my fingers drumming on the wheel. The same thing happened at the next light. And the next. Three yellow lights in a row. Was it a warning?

When I reached Isabella Street, I was grateful for the gridlock. It gave me time to look for numbers on the stores that I passed. I had no idea what sort of building 38 Isabella would be. But I did not expect a stately Victorian home, with grey-painted bricks and gingerbread trim.

I parked curbside, bought ninety minutes' parking from the Parking Authority machine, and laid the ticket on my dashboard. One hour and a half would be more than enough.

Crossing the street, I walked briskly. But my steps slowed as I approached the flagstone walk to the front door. Perhaps I should have a coffee first. Looking up the street, I saw a place called Java Jive on the next corner.

I entered Java Jive, bought a café latte and a pastry, and sank into a booth. This was procrastination. Mom had already filled me with bacon and eggs, toast and homemade strawberry jam. The pastry on the plate in front of me was stuffed with empty calories. Eating it, I felt a twinge of nausea. *This is ridiculous,* I told myself. *What's to fear? I'm just going into an office to fill out a form.* What was wrong with me? I'd never been this nervous before an examination or a job interview.

I gulped down the rest of my coffee and left Java Jive. Outside, sitting on the sidewalk beside a stuffed garbage bag, a female with dirty, matted hair held out an empty Styrofoam cup. I dropped in a loonie. The beggar looked up and muttered, "Thank you." I saw a pair of wide blue eyes and realized that she was only a girl. What was it that her eyes expressed? Not gratitude. Not indifference. More a feeling of baffled innocence so vulnerable it made me flinch.

As I waited to cross the street, a gleaming black Volvo, this year's model, cruised by. The driver was a pretty blonde. My eyes on the car, I stood like a boulder fixed in a riverbed while streams of pedestrians flowed around me. Finally I started across, and had to sprint the last few yards to the safety of the sidewalk.

Feeling feeble in the knees, I climbed the flagstone steps and opened the door.

"I think I've come to the right place," I said.

The receptionist smiled. She was young, brown-haired, with a round, placid face.

"If you want Adoption Services, this is it."

I took a deep breath.

"I'm a birth mother." The moment I said it, I felt my throat constrict. This was the first time I had used the word mother to define myself. "I believe there's a procedure for making contact with my child . . . a way to register?"

The smile faded, and she nodded gravely.

"Mary Flemming is the person you want to talk to. Her office is upstairs." The receptionist smiled again. "Good luck."

I took the stairs slowly, my hand on the banister, and stopped in front of the first open door. The office's only occupant looked up from her computer screen. She was a slim woman in her late thirties, with fine features and soft grey eyes.

"Mary Flemming?"

She nodded. When I had introduced myself and explained my purpose, she stood up.

"We have an interview room," she said. "It's more private."

After closing her office door, she led me down the hall to a small but comfortable lounge furnished with a sofa, various tables, and a swivel chair that faced the sofa. The sofa was for me, the swivel chair for her. She closed the door before sitting down.

While I explained that I wanted to find the child whom I had given up for adoption twenty-one years ago, she watched my face, nodding from time to time.

"Your daughter is part of your past," she said when I had finished. "If a reunion occurs, she will be part of your future, and you will be part of hers. To build a post-reunion relationship is a real challenge. You and your daughter each have your own personality, your own history, your own needs and desires. Have you thought about that?" She leaned back in her swivel chair, her eyes still bent upon mine. "Why do you want to meet her?"

I hesitated. "Partly I need to know how she is, how she turned out."

"The need to know. That's what brings most birth parents to us. Now I shall ask you the question I put to all of them. Are you asking for reassurance? Is it a reunion you need, or simply information? It's not fair to walk into someone's life, turn it upside down, and then walk out again."

I squirmed, tore my eyes from her cool, level gaze.

"I'm not married," I said. "I'm not in a stable relationship. Never have been. But out there somewhere is this person who is flesh of my flesh. If I find her, I'm not planning to walk out again."

"Do you have a fantasy about what it will be like? Something warm and cozy?"

I caught my breath. Ms. Flemming had nailed it. My daughter would look like me, or somewhat like me. Perhaps she would be a student. We would have a million things to talk about.

"What about the rest of your family?" Ms. Flemming continued. "Parents? Siblings? Do they know that you are registering to make contact with your child?"

"No one in my family knew that I was pregnant. Nor did the birth father."

"So you concealed the pregnancy. Why? Did you fear your family would reject you? That your boyfriend would abandon you?"

"At the time, I gave little thought to either possibility. All I wanted was to extricate myself and get on with my life. I was a student."

"I see." Her brows knit. "Well, it's not unusual to feel guilty."

Was she trying to put words into my mouth?

"I don't feel guilty."

"Don't you?" She glanced at her watch. "I have an appointment in five minutes. I'll get you some literature to read first. You don't have to register today. It's better to take this one step at a time."

For a moment I hesitated, knowing that if I didn't act now, perhaps I never would.

"Thank you," I said. "I'll gladly read the materials. But I do intend to register today."

Time had run out when I returned to the car. Seeing the meter maid advancing along the sidewalk, I felt lucky that there wasn't already a violation ticket under my wiper blade.

Plunging into the traffic on Yonge Street, I maneuvered my way north towards Highway 401. There was still time to escape the Toronto rush hour. I could stop to eat around Port Hope and reach Atherton before dark.

# Sixteen

"Socrates," I called, "where are you?"

The only thing waiting on the porch was a flyer from Giorgio's Pizza. Normally, whenever I went out, Socrates was at the front door ready to greet me on my return. This time it had been three days, the longest I had ever left him outdoors. The little black cat was nowhere to be seen.

I wasn't seriously worried. Though there was still plenty of light, the sun had set. Probably Socrates was already on the prowl. He was a savvy beast, able to take care of himself.

"Socrates!" I called again, half expecting him to materialize from the deep shadows under the shrubbery.

What I did not expect was the loud "Meow" from inside the house. And again, "Meow." Louder still. This was strange. He shouldn't be in the house. I hadn't left him in the house.

I tested the knob. The door was locked. Socrates meowed again. A cold feeling came over me, and my fingers fumbled as I searched in my handbag for the key, brushing my wallet and make-up bag before I found it. After inserting the key into the lock, I hesitated before turning the knob.

Picking up my suitcase, I stepped into the hall. Instantly, Socrates' furry body was twining about my ankles. He pushed the side of his face against my shin, purring hoarsely. I switched on the light. Everything looked normal. The house felt tight and airless after being shut up for three days. On the floor were two business envelopes and a travel brochure that had dropped through the mail slot. The hall clock ticked sonorously.

"Anybody here?" I shouted. My heart pounded. I was ready to bolt out the door if someone answered. Nobody did. The house felt empty. Yet I found myself peering around doorways as I went from room to room, through the living room, dining room and kitchen, then back to the front hall and up the stairs. I shivered at the sound of each squeaky tread. From the bathroom to the study, through both bedrooms I tiptoed, checking even the closets before returning downstairs.

Back in the kitchen, I noticed my spare house key still hanging in its usual place on the hook by the back door. My heart stopped thumping. I stooped to pet the cat.

"Socrates, I'm sorry. I didn't mean to shut you in the house."

But had I shut him in? I felt certain that I had not.

When I peered out the kitchen window, there was still enough light to see the saucers and the water bowl I had left on the back porch. At the sight of them, a clear picture flashed in my mind – Socrates gobbling his kibble. I had watched him polish off the second saucer just before I tried to phone Michael. Most certainly, the cat had been outside.

But had he sneaked in later? I knew from experience that Socrates could slip like a phantom through a door open only a few inches. Had he circled around to the front of the house and entered without my noticing before I finally locked up? There was no way to know.

My search yielded no signs of forcible entry. All the doors and windows remained locked. Nothing appeared to have been moved. Bookshelves, desk, dressing table, drawers, closets – all were as I had left them. Yet I could not shake the sense of disquiet, the niggling fear that somebody had been in my home.

Two voice mail messages were waiting. The first was from Michael, saying that he missed me and wanted me to phone as soon as I got home. The second was from Sebastian, announcing that he was ready to report.

I dithered about Michael. To phone or not to phone? I longed to see him, but I was sweaty, rumpled and tired after the long drive. If I called him, he might want to come over. This evening sex didn't interest me as much as a shower and early to bed – alone. Michael would have to wait.

As for Sebastian, the next day was Tuesday, the day we had fixed for him to report and to have his first tutorial. I phoned the Atherton Arms. When he did not answer his room phone, I hung up without leaving a message at the front desk. I could catch him in the morning.

Nursing a Scotch with extra ice, I tried to relax under the ceiling fan in the living room. The house felt somehow too empty, especially after Socrates insisted on going outdoors. I had let him go, acknowledging that he had friends to meet, territory to patrol, and rivals to challenge.

A siren wailed over on Main Street, four blocks away, reassuring me that Atherton's finest were on the job. To Serve and Protect. The siren also reminded me that I had to call the police station. Tonight? Maybe I should think about it first. If I called, should I report the intrusion? But how could I, when I wasn't sure that an intrusion had occurred? Agnew would assume that I had inadvertently left the cat in the house.

On the other hand, what if Agnew took my concern seriously? Then he would ask what an intruder might be looking for. I did have things to tell the Atherton police, but not that.

Sleepless most of the night, I tried to convince myself that no one had been in the house. But I'm no good at self-deception. Until two days ago, I had believed that George Pinkus and I were the only persons who knew about the manuscript. Thanks to Ken Hains, I now knew otherwise. If there were still more people who knew, and one of them had killed George, might he not also kill me?

I was awake when the first sounds of morning began to fill the darkness. Robins sang, sparrows cheeped, and the train rumbled through Atherton on its way from Toronto to Montreal. Dawn was breaking before I fully relaxed and fell into a deep sleep.

When I awoke, it was daylight. My bedside clock read 8:30. I got up, made coffee, and chewed my way through a bowl of granola. Then I phoned Sebastian. The phone rang three times before he answered.

"I'm still asleep," he said groggily.

"Do you know what time it is?"

"I don't care. Please let me sleep."

"It's nearly ten o'clock. I want to hear your report. Get up and get over here. And bring *The Canterbury Tales.* You have read The Prologue, haven't you?"

Sebastian groaned. "Oh, very well. See you in an hour."

I noticed that he had not answered my question. After hanging up, I pulled my own copy of Chaucer from the bookshelf, assuming Sebastian's groan meant that he had not completed his reading assignment. I hoped he had made better progress with his investigation into the scene of the crime.

Two hours later, Sebastian arrived on foot, carrying a clipboard and a copy of *Norton's Anthology of English Literature, Volume One.* He wore sneakers, a T-shirt and blue jeans, and his head was shorn in a buzz cut.

"You've gone native," I said. "Now you look like all the other students."

He ran his fingers through the blond stubble that covered his scalp. "No more hundred-dollar haircuts." He laughed ruefully. "Living rough might be amusing, so long as it doesn't last too long."

He flopped into an armchair, looking relaxed and comfortable until he noticed my copy of *The Canterbury Tales* on the coffee table.

I caught his apprehensive glance. "Chaucer is for later," I said, taking a seat on the sofa. "First, your report."

"Actually, it's rather gruesome."

"Don't spare me."

He rubbed his chin, looking as if he did not know how to begin. "My information came from Eddie, the desk clerk. The maid who actually found the body quit her job the same day. I couldn't have questioned her anyway, not unless I spoke Portuguese."

"What did you find out from the desk clerk?"

"Shall I start at the beginning?"

"That would seem reasonable."

He rubbed his chin again. "Well, the Atherton Arms checkout time is twelve noon. A few minutes before twelve, Pinkus went down to the lobby and asked if he could keep the room until one o'clock. Eddie said 'Okay.' Hotel guests often made that request. But Pinkus wanted to settle his bill immediately, which was a bit unusual. Eddie told him he could pay when he dropped off his key at the front desk after vacating the room. But Pinkus insisted. He was determined to pay right away. He said he would leave the key in the room when he left. The reason he gave was to save time later."

"It might have saved him two or three minutes," I acknowledged. But I guessed the real reason – George's fear that if he were to stop at the front desk on his way out, the clerk would notice the glint of metal at his wrist.

Sebastian continued. "The next thing Eddie noticed was a good-looking woman who came into the hotel carrying a briefcase. She looked around the lobby as if she owned the place."

"I was just wondering when was the last time anybody had cleaned the chandelier."

"So the woman was you. I thought as much. Well, you asked him to ring Pinkus' room to say you had arrived. That was at twelve noon. So Eddie knew that Pinkus was alive then."

"And the desk clerk saw me leave."

"Yes. About fifteen minutes later, carrying your briefcase, and with your nose in the air. Eddie said that nobody else came through the lobby. He hadn't left the desk the entire time, so he was certain about that. He didn't know that anything was wrong until he heard a woman's scream from somewhere on an upper floor. It wasn't just one scream. She was screeching non-stop. Eddie started up the stairs, because the elevator wasn't working, and followed the sound of shrieking all the way to the third floor. There he saw a maid standing outside Pinkus' room, with the door wide open. Apparently she was following her regular schedule and had gone in to clean. When she saw Eddie, she pointed at something in the room and kept on screaming. Eddie looked. There was Pinkus sprawled on the floor in a great pool of blood that had spread as far as the hall carpet." Sebastian paused. "About one metre from the body, Eddie saw a hand."

"A hand?"

"Pinkus' left hand, severed at the wrist."

I pictured the stubby fingers, the bone and gristle visible at the severed wrist.

Sebastian leaned forward. "Deirdre, are you all right? You look as though you might faint."

"No, no. I'm fine."

"You said not to spare you."

"Right." I took a deep breath. "Go on."

"You're sure?"

I nodded.

"Eddie called the manager, who hustled up from his office, took one look, and dialed 911 on his cell phone. The maid was still in hysterics when the police arrived. After they had taken a good look at the body, they said the victim had bled to death. There was a head wound too. It appeared that the murderer had clubbed the victim first, which meant he was unconscious when the killer hacked off his hand."

"Was there a briefcase in the room?" Even before asking, I was sure what the answer would be.

"A briefcase?" Sebastian's brow wrinkled. "I don't think so. Eddie didn't mention a briefcase. He said Pinkus had only one suitcase. It was closed, as if he'd been ready to leave when the killer stopped him."

"Was there anything else in the room that interested the police?"

"Such as?"

"Handcuffs?"

Sebastian blinked. "Surely not, or Eddie would have told me. According to him, the police found keys, a wallet, a comb, and an address book in the victim's pockets. That was all. One officer thought the murder had something to do with drugs. He wondered whether it might have been an execution, or maybe a warning to others. He thought the severed hand could be a sort of signature. You know, like in *The Scarlet Pimpernel.*"

"Hmm."

I knew better. Unexpectedly, I felt a stab of sympathy for poor unloved, unlucky George. The quickest way to get the briefcase was to chop off his hand. Amputation was faster than searching pockets for keys. If the killer wanted George to die, blood loss would do it. I wondered whether the killer had known in advance about the handcuffs. Or was his choice of murder weapon fortuitous? A knife. A cleaver. Maybe a hatchet.

Sebastian's report made me one hundred percent sure that the killer was after the briefcase, and ninety percent sure that he expected the manuscript to be in it. No doubt he was happy to find my twenty-five thousand dollars. But it was the manuscript he wanted. And he didn't have it yet.

A shiver passed through me. I leaned back against the sofa cushions and tried to think clearly. Did the killer know that I had the manuscript? How could he know? Maybe from Eddie? If the desk clerk was involved, it might have been he who tipped off the killer. I had given Eddie my name. Finding out where I lived would not have been difficult. So the killer might have been the intruder – if there was an intruder – in my home.

Sebastian regarded me thoughtfully. "Well, that's my report. I can't think of anything else I learned."

"You did very well. Thank you." I gave myself a shake. "Now shall we talk about Chaucer?"

"I'm ready," Sebastian said. From the look on his face, you would think he was ready to have a tooth pulled. Instead of opening his *Norton Anthology,* he crossed to the sofa and sat beside me. I opened my book to the Prologue to *The Canterbury Tales.*

"Okay," I said. "Start reading. Aloud."

"I can't read that Old English."

"First of all, it's Middle English. Second, yes you can. And if you're going to pass this course, you must."

He sighed, groaned, and obeyed:

When that Aprille with his shoures soote
The droughte of Marche hath perced to the roote,
And bathed every veyne in swich licour
Of which vertu engendered is the flour

"Flour?" Sebastian questioned.

"Think French."

*"Fleur?"*

"You've got it."

As we moved along, Sebastian really did get it. He took greater interest in Chaucer than I had expected, especially when we read the portrait of the Squire. This youth, "A lovyere and a lusty bachelor," truly did resonate with him. Well, they had much in common.

At one point during the lesson, Sebastian's hand migrated down my back. I moved from the sofa to the chair that he had vacated. After that, he focussed better. We had ploughed halfway through the Prologue to *The Canterbury Tales* by the time the tutorial ended.

After Sebastian had left, I called Michael to tell him that I was back.

"Good," he said. "How was Toronto?"

"I didn't see much of it. I was visiting my mother."

"An emergency? Until I got your message, I didn't realize you were going out of town."

"It was a spur-of-the-moment idea. When you know me longer, you'll realize how impetuous I can be."

"Are you subject to sudden urges?" He sounded amused.

"Sometimes."

"So am I. This time, an urge to see you."

"Great," I said. "Come for dinner."

It wasn't until I had hung up that I assessed the state of my food supplies. The box of spaghetti and jar of tomato sauce in the kitchen cupboard weren't much to offer. If I didn't do better than that, Michael might get the impression that I didn't know how to cook. A quick dash to the supermarket was needed. Lamb chops decorated with a sprig of parsley always look good on a plate. Boiled carrots are easy, and mashed potatoes safe. And of course, a bottle of wine. Any meal is better with Merlot.

As it turned out, I didn't have to cook. Michael arrived at six, carrying a shopping bag that contained a carton of eggs, a loaf of fresh bread, and a bag of mixed salad vegetables.

"What's this for?" I asked.

"I'm going to prepare an omelet, unless you have something else planned."

"Not really," I said, more than ready to let him show off his skills. "How will your omelet go with a glass or two of Merlot?"

"Superbly."

There is something sensual about watching a man cook an omelet. It is an invitation to intimacy. Men who make omelets intuitively sense the sexiness of the egg. When seduction is the goal, I'll bet that omelets score higher than flowers or chocolates.

Relaxing on a kitchen chair with my chin propped on my fists, I watched Michael's slender fingers crack the egg, beat it, and slide it into the oiled pan. I wanted those fingers on my body. But the omelet had to come first, with salad, bread and wine. Better not to rush things. The evening would advance in a pleasant progression that ultimately led to bed.

After dinner, we carried snifters of brandy out to the porch and settled on the swing. A cricket chirped in the bushes. Nighthawks swooped in the darkening sky. The streetlights came on. The scent of lilacs wafted from the garden. I gave a push with my feet to set the swing in motion, and then, resting my head on Michael's shoulder, gave myself up to the mingled pleasure of his nearness and the perfumed air.

Michael asked me about my family, and I talked about my mother's courage in dealing with my father's long illness. I told him about my sister Sheila, and about the happier days we had shared when there were four of us, and about the sense of loss that had been part of my life since Sheila died.

"Did your parents encourage you to go to grad school?" Michael asked.

"My father did, but not my mother. They both wanted me to go to university. But Mom expected me to graduate with an engagement ring as well as a degree. She often lets me know that my sister would have given her grandchildren."

"That could be annoying."

"It is."

"But you still visit her."

"She *is* my mother."

"This time, did you have any other reason to go to Toronto?"

Surprised at the question, I turned my head and found him studying me.

"Isn't visiting my mother a good enough reason?" I countered. When my eyes met his, I had the oddest feeling that he knew there was more.

When we had finished our brandy, we went inside. He stood watching me put dishes into the dishwasher. Then he came up behind me as I washed the omelet pan in the sink, and he circled me in his arms. When he laid the side of his face against my cheek, I breathed in the scent of sandalwood – much sexier than those musky men's colognes that are said to turn women on. At the feel of his skin, I felt shivery all the way down to my toes.

"I have a sudden urge," I said as I turned around in his arms and pulled him close.

When I woke at dawn, I propped myself on one elbow, looked down at Michael's sleeping face and wished that I could tell him everything. My habit of secrecy did not bode well for a long-term relationship. But how could I tell Michael about George Pinkus without explaining about the manuscript? How could I tell him about the intruder without disclosing what the intruder might have been after? Like it or not, *Cardenio* was the hidden centre of my life.

If it weren't for that manuscript, I might invite Michael to move in with me. Maybe not yet, but our affair would head in that direction if I let it. I leaned over and kissed his mouth, dreaming of romantic nights and leisurely breakfasts. Maybe his repertoire extended beyond omelets. It would be wonderful to have a live-in lover who could cook.

# Seventeen

By eight in the morning, Michael had left. It was discouraging to have my lover leap so determinedly from my bed, yet I admired his self-discipline. To keep regular office hours even during summer was a practice I'd never been able to sustain. My way was to work through the night when I felt like it, then sleep until noon. On those occasions when I had a man in my bed, I wasn't fussy about getting to work at all. With a twinge of regret, I rolled over and patted the hollow in the pillow where Michael's head had been and where the scent of sandalwood lingered.

I showered, dressed, and grabbed a cherry-bottom yogurt from the fridge. Sitting at the kitchen table stirring the yogurt, I reviewed my plans for the day. Sebastian was not coming for his daily session until the afternoon. I had to phone Detective Agnew. When the police heard what I'd learned about George's past, they'd surely start looking at other suspects besides me. But the suspicion that an intruder had been in my home while I was away, combined with Sebastian's report, had dealt a blow to my revenge theory. Whether they were connected or not, neither supported the idea that George's death was linked to his pedophilia. I felt deflated. And scared.

A sudden movement outside the window caught my eye. Socrates had leapt onto the sill. Through the glass I saw a tiny yellow feather stuck to his whiskers. I rapped on the glass.

"Bad cat!"

Why couldn't he stick to sparrows and leave the goldfinches alone? I let him in. While cleaning his whiskers he watched me slurp my yogurt. Socrates looked pleased with himself – the opposite of the way I felt.

I rinsed out the yogurt carton and put it into the recycling bin while contemplating what to do first. Phone Detective Agnew, or finish reading Cervantes' version of the Cardenio story? Cervantes won the toss. I wanted to get the source, the original story, set firmly in my mind before starting on the play. My phone call to Detective Agnew could wait until later in the day.

Climbing the stairs resolutely, I took *Don Quixote* and my pad of yellow paper into the study and sat down at my desk. My bookmark was at the page where I had left off. Cardenio had just promised to find Fernando and force him to marry Dorotea. Now what?

I flipped through the next six chapters. Nothing seemed to be happening. It was as if Cervantes had forgotten about the Cardenio/Luscinda, Fernando/Dorotea story just as it was reaching its climax. The characters were still there, but busily solving Don Quixote's problems to the complete neglect of their own. Curiously, Cardenio had been restored to sanity. Cervantes seemed to have forgotten about his main character's madness as well as about the plot.

At Chapter Thirty-Six, Cervantes picked up Cardenio's saga again, as four armed horsemen wearing black masks arrived at the inn where Don Quixote and his companions were staying. With them, under guard, was a woman veiled in white.

Before I learned who she was or what fate the men planned for her, my phone rang. I recognized Detective Agnew's deep voice.

"Good morning, Dr. Gunn. So you're back in town?"

"Good morning," I said. "I was going to call you today. I have something to tell you."

"Fine. You can do that when you get to the station. We have more questions to ask. This time officially."

I thought about Constable Montour hunched over her notebook, writing as fast as her pen could fly. If that wasn't official, what was?

Putting away *Don Quixote,* I changed into a paisley skirt and blue silk blouse. Classy but toned-down. Except for lipstick, I applied no makeup beyond concealer to mask the purple smudges under my eyes. If you look exhausted, it's impossible to project an image of complete control.

I'm not sure what I expected to see when Agnew escorted me through the door of the interview room. Maybe something like a cell, with a hard stool for me to sit on and a spotlight to shine on my face. Instead, I saw comfortable chairs pulled up around a table, and drapes on the windows. The tape recorder was the only object that matched my expectations.

An older man, about sixty, was already seated. He had silver hair, neatly combed, and faded blue eyes behind rimless glasses. Rising slightly, he introduced himself as Detective Inspector Boothby, and sat down as I took a seat. Both officers were in plain clothes. Constable Montour was not present. The atmosphere was calm and serious.

That suited me.

I prayed to God that the police did not know that I had withdrawn twenty-five thousand dollars from my Registered Retirement Savings Plan. If they did, they would demand the reason. And if I didn't provide a plausible explanation, Agnew would cling all the more tightly to the blackmail theory and my name would stay at the top of his list.

The tape machine clicked on, I took a deep breath and thought: Here we go!

"This is Detective Agnew. With me are Detective Inspector Boothby and Dr. Deirdre Gunn. It's Wednesday, July 5. The time is 11:45 a.m."

Full eye contact. A slight leaning forward. Agnew was on home turf. He had the upper hand.

Stay cool, I told myself. Don't reveal more than you have to.

Agnew got right to the point. "Dr. Gunn, on Friday, June 23, you withdrew twenty-five thousand dollars from your RRSP. Between 11:30 and 11:45 a.m. you picked up the money from your bank, in cash. At 12:00 p.m., you visited George Pinkus' room at the Atherton Arms Hotel, carrying a briefcase."

Oh shit! They knew about the money. If they had not known, I would have said – but only if asked – that my briefcase contained notes for a book I was writing and that I had it with me because I was on my way to the library to do research. But I couldn't use that story now. The time frame spoke loud and clear, and it spoke against me. Like it or not, I had to tell them about the manuscript.

Agnew continued, "Do you want to explain?"

"No."

Within my own professional experience, I'd grilled dozens of students. Whether the suspected offence was plagiarism, buying essays on the Internet, or cheating on an examination, I recognized a guilty face when I saw one. So did Agnew and Boothby.

Boothby spoke for the first time. His voice was patient, yet firm – the voice of a man who had no time for lies or excuses. "Did you take the twenty-five thousand dollars to Mr. Pinkus?"

"Yes." I slumped in my seat.

"Please repeat that. The tape recorder may not have picked up what you said."

Raising my head, I spoke up clearly. "The money was in my briefcase. Cash. Bundles of fifty-dollar bills. I took it to George. I gave him the money. Then I left."

"Blackmail," Agnew grunted. "I knew it from the start."

"Please." Boothby held up a hand. "I would like Dr. Gunn to explain this without interruption. Continue please, Dr. Gunn."

Beneath the table, my fingers twisted the fabric of my skirt.

"George had got hold of the manuscript of an old play. Early Seventeenth Century. Its value depended on historical context. He saw the possibility that William Shakespeare had written it. Was it authentic? Was its existence previously known? He brought it to my home for me to examine because he knew I had the expertise to find answers to those questions. He had offered me a partnership, and I thought we had a deal. But then he said I needed to put up one hundred thousand dollars. I told him I didn't have the money, and without a job, I couldn't borrow it. He said it looked like we didn't have a deal after all. He put the manuscript back in his briefcase and started to leave. I followed him out to the front porch." I paused. "My neighbours across the street saw us arguing. They've told you about that."

Agnew's face showed no response.

I continued, "Afterwards, over the phone, we haggled. When I made clear that twenty-five thousand was as high as I could go, he said he would take it."

Agnew's face went red. There had been no blackmail. No compromising photographs. His theory had been shot to pieces. He hunched forward, glaring at me. "A manuscript! Why in God's name didn't you tell us this to start with?"

Boothby leaned back in his chair. I could see him coolly dissecting my story. "Did Pinkus ask for the money in cash?"

"He did."

"Didn't that make you suspicious?"

"I didn't worry about it."

He regarded me in silence. I began to sweat.

"You might have wondered how Pinkus had obtained the manuscript."

"The question did occur to me. But it was a once-in-a-lifetime opportunity. I was willing to take a chance."

"The slim chance that it actually belonged to him? You surprise me, Dr. Gunn. As a scholar, wouldn't you need to know the history of the manuscript, how it passed from one person to another. What do you call that? Providence?"

"Provenance."

"Thank you." He took off his glasses, wiped them carefully, then put them back on. "You have the manuscript in your care at present?"

"Yes. It's in my safety deposit box at the bank."

"You may be asked to surrender it as material evidence. Be sure that it remains in your possession as long as this investigation continues."

"It will."

Detective Agnew clicked off the tape recorder.

"Just a minute," I protested. "I have something to say. When I was in Toronto, I talked to several people who know a lot about George Pinkus. You need to hear what they told me."

He clicked the machine back on and let me talk without interruption. Neither policeman looked impressed.

After turning off the tape recorder, Inspector Boothby said, "Several of Mr. Pinkus' victims as well as their parents testified at his trial. The Toronto police will interview all of them, if they haven't already. I'll pass on the information that you just gave us. But whatever you may think, revenge killing of pedophiles is rare.

"Greed is a more common motive. In the light of what you've told us, it seems probable that the killer came to Pinkus' hotel room to get the manuscript, not knowing that Pinkus had already parted with it."

I nodded. "That's my fear."

"No doubt the killer was happy to receive a gift of twenty-five thousand dollars. But he still doesn't have the manuscript." Boothby frowned. "I'm no expert on literature, Dr. Gunn. But I've noticed that the Shakespeare industry is big business. Remember that portrait that turned up in Ottawa a few years ago? The same family had held onto it for four centuries. They claimed it was a picture of Shakespeare that one of their ancestors had painted."

"You mean the so-called Sanders' portrait?"

"That's right. And a couple of months ago I read in the newspaper that a copy of Shakespeare's *First Folio* fetched nearly six million dollars at a London auction."

"Yes. That was close to the expected price."

"So it seems to me, Dr. Gunn, that a lost play would be a huge find. Somebody like you could use it to snag a position at a top-ranking university. There'd be fortunes made. Collectors. Publishers. Agents. You know better than I how many people would like a piece of something like that."

"Exactly." I couldn't have expressed it better myself.

"I'd be careful," he said, "if I were you."

# Eighteen

A sultry night. Crickets chirped in the bushes outside my open windows. I had hoped to catch a breeze, but the only air movement was what the ceiling fan in the living room stirred up. Socrates lay beside me on the sofa while I wrote up my notes on the final episode of Cardenio's tale, as told by Cervantes.

- Four masked men and a veiled lady arrive at inn.
- The men are taking her to a nunnery against her will.
- Cardenio recognizes Luscinda's voice.
- The mask slips from the face of the man restraining her. He is Fernando.
- Dorotea recognizes Fernando. She faints.
- Fernando recognizes Dorotea and Cardenio.
- Luscinda beseeches Fernando to let her go to her true husband, Cardenio.
- Dorotea beseeches Fernando to remember his promise to marry her.
- Luscinda recognizes Cardenio and is overcome with joy.
- Fernando accepts his responsibility to marry Dorotea.
- The end.

Apparently Cardenio and Luscinda, Fernando and Dorotea will live happily every after. Ah, well. In romance, anything can happen. Shakespeare turned other implausible plots into great theatre. *The Tempest. The Winter's Tale.* He could do it, if anyone could. Soon I'd find out. Now that I knew the basic source material, I was ready to tackle the manuscript. It was time to retrieve it from my safety deposit box.

The hall clock chimed eleven. I rose from the sofa.

"Socrates, it's time for you to go out."

He stretched, jumped from the seat, and was ambling toward the front door when a twig snapped just outside, in the shrubbery under the window. Socrates stopped, one paw raised, and swivelled his ears in the direction of the sound. No raccoon, skunk or cat would make that sharp a noise. It had to be a human prowler, with heavy feet. A cold chill ran down my spine.

Socrates glanced up at me, as if seeking confirmation, then continued into the front hall, where he stood beside the door, waiting. I took a quick look at the lock. Yes, the bolt was in place.

"Not on your life, cat. You're staying in the house tonight."

Socrates meowed plaintively.

"Use your kitty litter. I'm not opening that door."

I visualized an intruder the size of a football linebacker hurling himself through the entrance, demanding the manuscript.

After giving me a baleful look, Socrates stalked down to the basement.

If only Michael were here, instead of living on the other side of town. Well, why not call him? Atherton is a small city. He could be here in twenty minutes. I picked up my phone and punched his number. After four rings, the answering service cut in. Michael's voice promised that he would return my call as soon as possible.

That couldn't be soon enough.

"Michael," I babbled, "I think someone is prowling outside. Could you come over? Please. Spend the night? Even if it's two in the morning when you get this message, I need you here."

Of course it wouldn't be two in the morning. Knowing Michael's conscientious habits, I was sure he'd be home any minute. Then he would get my message and call me. Or drive straight over without phoning.

I locked all the windows and doors.

Half an hour later, still no word from Michael. He didn't have a cellphone. Maybe I should try his office. He might be working late. I punched the number. No luck.

I looked out the living room window, then the kitchen window. Saw nothing. Probably I should phone a neighbour. But I didn't know my neighbours well, except maybe Harold and Alma. Harold could swing his cane at the prowler. That sure would scare the pants off him!

I wished I had a gun. I wished Socrates were a Great Dane. I wished Michael would hurry to my rescue. I didn't want to call 911, or do anything to attract still more attention from the police.

The closest thing to a weapon was the poker in the fire-tools stand. With its spear-like tip and its sharp hook at right angles to the shaft, it even looked like a weapon. I took it from the stand, tested its heft. Holding it more or less like a baseball bat, I tried a couple of practice swings.

Socrates, back from the litter box, eyed me scornfully. A cat recognizes a chicken when it sees one. We both knew I could never steel myself to swing that poker at another human being. Better phone 911. I couldn't wait for Michael one more minute.

Sirens wailed, lights flashed, and brakes squealed at the curb. I expected the police to come quickly. But thirty seconds! A big surprise. On my way to the front door, I glanced out the window in time to see a bent-over figure with a pair of skinny legs scissor up my driveway in the direction of the back fence.

The policeman sprinted up the porch steps. I had the door open before he had time to ring the bell. Facing me was a young man. Early thirties. An open, friendly face.

"That was quick," I said, "but not quick enough. Whoever it was jumped the back fence."

"Did you get a look at him?"

"Thin. Probably young. He ran like a kid."

"Likely was a kid. There's a theft ring that uses kids operating around here. They target a car, then get a kid to steal it. Kid gets a thrill and a few bucks. He takes the rap if he's caught. But he's a young offender. No big deal. The car goes to a chop shop."

The officer turned his head in the direction of my driveway, where my ten-year-old BMW sat unmolested. "Thieves don't usually bother with those kind – not that old, anyway."

"I don't think he was after my car."

"You live alone?"

I nodded.

"We been getting a lot of home invasions lately. You should get a friend to stay with you."

"I'm working on it."

"For your safety, do it. There are some bad characters around." He handed me his card. ATHERTON POLICE SERVICE P.C. Peter Radley #28. "Call any time you need us."

"Are you always this fast? You got here in thirty seconds."

"We're keeping an eye on your place. Maybe you haven't noticed, but a patrol drives by every hour."

"Really?" I attempted a smile. "That makes me feel safer."

As soon as Constable Radley had left, I freed Socrates into the night. Did I *really* feel safer, knowing that the Atherton police were keeping an eye on me? Up to a point. But it meant one of two things. Either I was still a suspect, or the police thought I was in danger. Neither alternative was reassuring.

With the windows shut and no central air, the house felt like a sauna. I went up to my bedroom, stripped, and flopped naked on top of my bedspread. The blades of the small fan on my dresser rattled noisily. Between the clatter of the fan and the thoughts racing through my brain, I got little sleep.

As soon as it was light, I opened the windows to let in the morning breeze. After showering, I went down to the kitchen. Socrates had not come home. I brewed coffee, made toast, and then sat at the kitchen table to eat.

Sebastian arrived at ten o'clock for his daily tutorial. I was glad to see a friendly, non-threatening human being. I showed him into the living room, where he settled into an armchair facing the sofa, ready if not eager to learn.

I was pleased with Sebastian. He had been making progress – more than I'd dared to expect. Unlike those students whose only concern is to soak up what the instructor says and then wring it out for the final exam, he was not a sponge. True, he was lazy; but he had opinions, although sometimes they were not well grounded. I found it exciting to see his mind grab onto a new idea. He was improving with age.

Since I began tutoring Sebastian, we had progressed from Chaucer to Shakespeare. The assigned play was *Hamlet,* which Sebastian acknowledged to be rather good. He thought that Laertes was a fine chap, Hamlet too introspective, and Ophelia not sexy enough.

"The examiner won't care whether you want to hang out with Laertes or date Ophelia," I said sternly. "Concentrate on how Shakespeare develops the plot, and what the plot reveals about the characters. Think about the moral issues in the play."

He sucked the end of his ballpoint reflectively. "Gertrude is fascinating. She's a lot like you, isn't she?" His eyes sparkled as he said this. "Plenty of firepower under the bonnet. I'm sure she has auburn hair."

So far, this was the closest he had come to expressing a literary judgment.

During the tutorial, the post had arrived. As Sebastian was leaving, I picked up the letter that had dropped through the mail slot. The envelope, addressed to me in unfamiliar handwriting, bore no return address. I was intrigued. Anything that's handwritten deserves attention. I carried the letter into the living room, sat down, and tore open the envelope.

The letter was written on a single sheet of paper. It began, "Hi Deirdre," I glanced down the page to where it ended, "Better take care/ Love, Ken."

This was odd. Ken had my phone number and e-mail address; so why had he gone to the trouble of looking up my postal address? Nobody used snail mail any longer.

In his first sentence, Ken explained:

"I didn't phone because the police may have a tracer on the line. And I didn't e-mail because they might seize my computer. It seems that I recently threatened to kill George. Honestly, I don't remember exactly what I said to him, but I did go to his apartment about a month ago to try to get back a $200 advance on a rare book that he had promised to purchase for me. The occupant of the next apartment heard me yelling at George through the wall. The two apartments share the third floor of an old house near Kensington Market, with some pretty flimsy drywall to separate them. Anyway, this worthy citizen felt it was his duty to report the incident. So I too am now a person of interest, or whatever they call it.

"Deirdre, you'd better not respond to this letter. Destroy it. And don't try to get in touch until this mess blows over.

We don't want the police to think that you and I are in cahoots."

My hands, still holding the letter, dropped to my lap. Well, well! What to make of this? I leaned my head against the chair back and closed my eyes. How did Ken's letter connect with the red pen I had picked up from the floor of his flat? 'Bide Your Time Budget Motel/Atherton, Ontario.'

Perhaps there was no connection. It is in the nature of pens to travel about, moving in mysterious ways from one person's pocket to another person's handbag. It could be a coincidence that a pen from Atherton reached its journey's end in Toronto. But I needed to know. Had Ken visited Atherton, or not?

If I could believe Ken, George had tried to sell him the *Cardenio* manuscript six weeks ago, and Ken had turned him down. But afterwards, did Ken reconsider? Maybe he decided that he did want the manuscript. Wanted it a lot. Maybe he tried to get in touch with George, only to learn that George had gone to Atherton. In that case, Ken might have suspected that George had gone to meet a potential buyer here. Hence a quick trip, aiming to reach him before a deal could be completed. Plausible? Not really. But possible. In retrospect, I detected a note of insincerity in Ken's voice when he told me that he had never been to Atherton. And he had changed the subject fast.

I'd better look into this, I thought as I carried the letter upstairs. Too hastily I tore it to pieces and flushed it down the toilet as Ken had advised me to do. As the last scrap of paper disappeared in a swirl of water, it suddenly occurred to me that I should have kept the letter until I had checked whether Ken had been in Atherton at the time of George's murder.

The simplest approach was to inspect the Bide Your Time's register. In a mystery novel, this would be a job for a private detective. A gumshoe. But that would cost money. And I was confident that I could handle the search on my own. I would present myself as a businesswoman, I decided. How should I dress? I would carry my briefcase, of course. But the Bide Your Time Budget Motel was not a Holt Renfrew sort of place.

From the back of my closet I dragged out a lime-green pantsuit that had been in style five years ago. It had fit better then, I thought ruefully as I tugged on the pants. When all this was over, I'd better start working out at the gym.

The Bide Your Time Budget Motel was located on the outskirts of town, on a secondary highway that connected a series of Eastern Ontario communities, strung like beads on a necklace along the north shore of the St. Lawrence River. It was a single-storey building, pink stucco with a neon sign advertising budget rooms with TV and air conditioning – a home away from home for struggling salesmen and desperate lovers. At two in the afternoon, the only car parked in front of a unit was an aging Taurus wagon that needed a wash.

Inside the office, a nondescript, fiftyish woman wearing a blue cardigan sat at the desk. Her hair was black, with white roots visible at the part. When she glanced up, pencilled eyebrows raised, she could see that I carried no luggage.

"How may I help you?"

"I need a receipt for Income Tax purposes. I stayed here for one night, on business, about a month ago. I paid cash, and got a receipt. But I've lost it. I'd appreciate it if you could provide a duplicate ... My name is Diane Grant." I plunked my briefcase rather ostentatiously on the counter, hoping that she would notice the gold-embossed initials on the brown leather.

Her thin lips pressed together in a straight line. "I don't remember you, but I'm only here until 6:00, when my husband takes over." Eyeing me doubtfully, she pulled the register toward her. It was a big, black book with lined pages.

"What date did you stay?"

"It was either the twenty-second or the twenty-third of June," I said, naming the day before George's murder as well as the day itself. "I can't remember exactly."

She flipped back a few pages and then, starting at the top, ran the tip of a ballpoint down the column.

"Diane Grant," she mumbled. "Nope. Can't find you here."

"Let me look. Maybe I can find it." Before she could object, I seized the register and turned it around so that I could read the entries.

The open page was headed June 22. Quickly I scanned the list and there, nearly at the bottom, was the name I sought: Kenneth J. Hains.

The woman grabbed the book back.

"This is confidential," she spluttered. "You have no right –"

"Sorry. I just wanted to help you out. So few can read my handwriting."

Tight-lipped, she slammed the register shut.

"I didn't see my name," I said calmly. "Must have been some place else I stayed. These sorts of places all look alike, don't they?"

Her eyes locked on mine. She knew she'd been had. Through gritted teeth she muttered. "It's an unusual mistake."

She won't mention this to her husband, I thought as I smiled and walked away. She won't want him to know she was gulled so easily.

"Thanks anyway," I said as I opened the door. All the way back to my car, I felt her eyes watching me.

I drove away quickly, hoping that it hadn't occurred to her to take my licence plate number – not that it would matter very much.

So my old pal had lied to me. Ken the poet. Ken the rare book lover. Ken the liar. Was he also Ken the killer? I still did not want to believe it. But if he had not come to Atherton in pursuit of the manuscript, what was his reason? The fact that he had used his real name suggested that he had nothing to hide. Or it might mean that he found himself forced to pay by credit card and had no choice.

Having proof of his lie, I could not trust his letter. But what lay behind that letter? Why had he lied?

# Nineteen

The next day, after Sebastian's tutorial, I drove downtown to the bank to retrieve *Cardenio* from my safety deposit box. Now that I had completed my summary of the source material, I was ready to tackle the play itself, and with no time to waste. To copy out a five-act play by hand would require many days. I needed to finish my transcription before Agnew showed up with a warrant to seize the manuscript.

The young bank clerk, who was all of five-foot-one, had to fetch a stool to reach my safety deposit box, and even then it was a stretch. After unlocking a tiny metal door, she pulled mine from the wall of numbered boxes, handed it down to me and climbed off the stool.

"Take all the time you need," she said, and showed me into a room no larger than a closet. "When you finish, come and get me. I'll be out front." She switched on a fluorescent light. One of its two tubes flashed luridly, and hummed.

Having closed the door, I set the grey metal box on a grey metal table, removed the cover, and lifted out the manuscript. Unwrapped, it resembled something dead and mummified. Was this an illusion? By fluorescent light, I look mummified too. But I didn't remember the manuscript appearing this ancient when I put it into the vault only a couple of weeks ago.

Without being an expert on manuscript preservation, I knew that a metal box in an airless vault was no place to store a fragile document. What it needed was a specialized HVAC System – Heating, Ventilation and Air Conditioning. However and wherever *Cardenio* had spent its first three hundred years, the past century must have taken a heavy toll. After decades of neglect in the King's College stacks, it had undergone twenty years of George Pinkus' dubious stewardship. Without climate control, it would not last much longer.

I placed my forefinger gently on the first page. Good rag paper. Then I lowered my nose and sniffed. Dust. And behind that, a sharp, dry smell. Moving my lips silently, I read the opening lines:

> *Cardenio.* These seven days spent from home have now undone
> My peace forever.
>
> *Pedro.* Good, be patient, sir.
>
> *Cardenio.* She is my wife by contract before Heaven
> And all the angels, sir.
>
> *Pedro.* I do believe you;
> But where's the remedy now? Luscinda's gone.
> Fernando hath possession.

The words carried me down the tunnel of centuries, to a man sitting at a wooden table in a low-ceilinged room where a candle threw disproportionate shadows upon a roughcast plaster wall. In front of the man lay a sheet of vellum.

The man was about fifty, plump and slightly bald. His eyes were shrewd, but tired, his thoughts preoccupied with a story still trapped in his head. The pen in his hand was a quill – the sharpened feather of a bird. He dipped it in the inkpot. He wrote.

Outside the tiny room where I sat, footsteps moved. There was a sudden clunk as somebody's safety deposit box was shoved back into its opening, then the clang of a metal door slamming shut. The footsteps receded. I looked back at the manuscript, but the man with the pen had gone.

Yet the words remained, words written four hundred years ago. I had to take care of those words.

Atherton's sole expert on manuscript preservation was Nancy Bold, a librarian at the Melrose University Library. Trained as a conservator of ancient documents, Nancy was wasted at Melrose, which possessed little in the way of special collections. The Archives' oldest document dated back a mere century and a half, to the founding of the university.

Nancy was English, transported from Britain when her biologist husband accepted a position at Melrose. Having worked at the London Metropolitan Archives, which house records going back to the fifteen hundreds, Nancy sniffed at the Canadian notion of old.

Not since the day my employment ended had I set foot on campus. Nor did I want to. I wouldn't have gone near the place if I hadn't needed Nancy's advice.

Three dollars deposited in a machine bought an hour in the Visitors' Parking Lot. The faculty sticker still glued to my windshield would have given me free parking in the lot behind the Arts Building, but I didn't want to meet anyone I knew.

Leaving the car, I squared my shoulders, ready to face the stares of the curious. But not one of the dozen or so people walking toward me on the sidewalk gave me a glance. I might have been any middle-aged female academic, briefcase in hand, heading toward the university library. Nor did anyone pay any heed as I mounted the university library's worn limestone steps and pulled open the heavy oak door. This lack of attention was reassuring and disconcerting at the same time. It is not pleasant to be overlooked.

At the Information Desk, a spotty young man with a large Adam's apple, and wearing a gold ring in his ear, barely lifted his head. Was Professor Gunn already yesterday's news?

"You'll find Ms. Bold at the desk in the Second Floor Reading Room," he said in answer to my inquiry.

I met no one on the staircase. The Reading Room was empty except for one male student, asleep with his head on his folded arms at one of the massive oak tables, snoring loudly.

Nancy Bold, a stocky woman with pallid skin, thick glasses and iron-grey hair was alone at the desk. She looked up from her computer screen.

"Hello, Deirdre, what may I do for you?" From the tone of her voice, I might have been in the Reading Room the day before, and nothing had happened at all. It felt good to be there.

"I have a question about manuscript conservation."

Her eyes brightened behind her thick lenses. This was something right up her alley.

"What is your question?"

"If you had a rare old manuscript in your personal collection, where would you keep it?"

"How old?"

"Seventeenth century."

Nancy frowned. "I wouldn't keep it anywhere. I would sell or donate it to a library that could provide the proper conditions of temperature, ventilation and humidity." The way she eyed my briefcase suggested that the manuscript was beaming secret signals in her direction. An S.O.S. But I suppressed the impulse to show it to her. The fewer people who knew about *Cardenio,* the better.

"I agree one hundred per cent. But if you happened to be working at home on such a manuscript, where would you keep it. Temporarily, of course."

"In the refrigerator."

"Seriously?"

"The refrigerator is not ideal, but it's more suitable than the desk drawer where you probably keep it now."

"What part of the fridge? Does it matter?"

"Not the meat compartment. Too cold. Or the vegetable crisper. Too humid. I don't suppose you own a psychrometer?"

"A what?" It sounded like something a psychiatrist might use to measure patients.

She looked at me as if I were either mentally defective or morally culpable. "A psychrometer is a thermometer with a dry bulb and a wet bulb for measuring atmospheric humidity."

"I'm afraid not," I said sheepishly.

"Well, a hydrometer serves the same purpose. It measures relative humidity. You can buy a hydrometer at a hardware store. Don't let the RH in your refrigerator get above forty-five percent. Your refrigerator will have some way to control humidity. Keep it low. While you're actually working with the manuscript, avoid light and dust. You should wear thin cotton gloves. If that isn't practical, be sure to wash your hands frequently. Skin oils damage old paper."

"Right," I said. "Thanks a lot."

On the way home I stopped at Pro Hardware to buy a waterproof pouch, as an extra precaution, and to order a hydrometer. They did not have one in stock.

*Cozy* wasn't a word I'd choose to describe a refrigerator. But there was something bright and cheerful about the array of fridge magnets that enlivened the blank, white door. There was a miscellany, some magnets placed there by Professor Weaver, but most by me. Many were commercial, advertising the services of plumbers, electricians, travel agents, spas and hairdressers. Then there were the whimsical gifts from my friends who thought I might enjoy a pair of penguins or a small green frog. Held in place by the magnets were various notes to myself, reminders of appointments and lists of things to do.

The clutter on the door was nothing compared to the clutter within. In the main compartment three half-empty jars of mayonnaise jostled two of Dijon mustard and a very dry chunk of cheddar cheese. There were also an open box of baking soda, a carton of eggs, half a bottle of vermouth, and several containers of yogurt.

In the crisper lay a wilted fistful of green. Picking it up, I recognized the parsley I had bought the day after my return from Toronto. That was the day when I had planned to cook dinner for Michael, but he had prepared an omelet instead. The carrots I had bought were also there, black-spotted and mushy in their plastic bag. At least, I thought ruefully, I had remembered to put the lamb chops into the freezer.

I pulled out the crisper drawer and, after dumping its contents into the garbage bin, filled the sink with warm water to give the crisper a good scrub. When taking out the crisper, I had noticed under it an open space that looked about the size I needed. When I tried it, the manuscript, enclosed in the pouch, fit perfectly.

The crisper drawer was manufactured of clear plastic. But if I kept it full of fruits and vegetables, nobody could see what lay underneath. Who would think to look in such a place?

Michael and I faced each other across my kitchen table, sharing a mushroom omelet, a salad, and a bottle of Baco Noir. I wondered whether omelets were the only things he knew how to cook. Such narrowness of repertoire would be a disappointment, although he did omelets very well.

"By the way," I said, peering at him over the rim of my wine glass, "I'm tutoring Sebastian Pomeroy for the English

201 supplemental examination." I laughed. "Dr. Gunn's cram school."

His fork, with a chunk of mushroom on the tines, paused in mid-air.

"You're doing *what?*"

"Tutoring Sebastian. I thought I should tell you."

"Why would you want to help him?" Michael set down his fork.

"His father cut his allowance in half because he failed his year. He's working hard to redeem himself."

Michael observed me narrowly. "That's not your problem."

"No. But he deserves a second chance."

"Oh for Chrissake, Deirdre! How could you get involved with him again?"

"Involved? You mean sexually? Certainly not. By second chance I meant an opportunity to get a credit for English 201."

Michael's face hardened. "You're making a mistake. If you want my advice –"

"I don't." I lowered my wineglass to the table. "Let's say no more about Sebastian."

"How can you pity him?" Michael persisted. "After the trouble he caused you?"

"He's just a kid," I said lamely, knowing that I couldn't tell him about my bargain with Sebastian. Maybe someday, but not now.

We finished our meal in grumpy silence. When I offered coffee, I expected him to refuse. To my surprise, he accepted. By the time we had carried our mugs out to the porch, the frost was starting to melt.

Harold and Alma, wooden-faced, watched from their front porch.

"There's marriage for you," Michael said. "I'll bet those two haven't communicated except to needle each other for the past twenty years."

"Oh, I don't know. They seem quite contented."

"You don't see the signs. You've never been married."

"Granted."

"Then you can't know the horror of it."

Harold and Alma, side by side in their Muskoka chairs, looked perfectly congenial. What were the signs that I had missed?

"There are good marriages," I said. "While I was growing up, my parents had a great relationship. They sometimes bickered, but 'horror' was far from it."

He shrugged. "From my own experience, marriage isn't an institution I'd recommend."

"It's not for everybody," I asserted, trying to sound as if I agreed. Yet Michael's vehemence dealt a blow to my hopes for a permanent relationship.

"My marriage was a five-year jail sentence," he continued.

"That bad?"

"Christ, I couldn't leave the house without Monica wanting to know where I was going and when I'd be back. If I ran into friends and wanted to join them, I had to phone to tell her I wouldn't be home for dinner. And if she'd already started cooking it, there'd be hell to pay."

My sympathies inclined toward Monica, but I didn't say so.

"Marriage was prison," he continued. We ate at a certain time, went to bed at a certain time. Sex on Saturdays. Roast beef on Sundays. Christmas dinners alternated between her parents' house and mine."

"Most people follow some kind of schedule," I said, feeling defensive. "You do too."

"Yes, but it's *my* schedule, not one forced on me by somebody else." His mouth tightened to a thin line. "Seriously, Deirdre, would you settle for that kind of life?"

"Well, no," I said quickly. "I believe that relationships should be open and free."

"Monica didn't see it that way. We were facing our sixth Christmas when I made my break. 'I'm going to Puerto Rico to camp in the rainforest for two weeks,' I told her, 'and I'll see you after New Year's.' When I got back, she had gone home to mother."

"And you never saw her again?"

"It wasn't as clean as that. But I haven't seen her for a long time. For ten years she's been married to a doctor. They have four kids. Last time I phoned, she treated me like a telemarketer. 'No thanks. Not interested.'" Michael smiled. "Of course, her husband may have been in the room."

"Have you no regrets?"

"Regrets that I don't have a wife to run my life? Regrets that I don't have to get up at five every morning to take Junior to the hockey rink?"

His tone of voice put me off. I found myself wanting to stick up for the moms and dads who spend their weekends in some freezing arena with their butts on a hard bench watching peewee hockey. Time to change the subject, or at least steer it in a different direction.

"Where does Monica live?"

"In Toronto. Rosedale."

"I was there recently."

"When you visited your mother? I didn't realize she lived in Rosedale."

"She doesn't."

"So what were you doing there?"

I nearly choked. What business was it of his? We'd just been talking about freedom, and here he was questioning me. I was tempted to point this out, but checked myself.

"Calling on friends," I said.

He must have recognized his mistake. "Sorry. I didn't mean to pry."

I set down my coffee, determined to bring my irritation under control before it became real anger. "I'm sorry too. I've been grouchy all day. Too much on my mind."

He squeezed my hand. "Maybe you should tell me about it."

I attempted a smile. God knows I wanted to confide in him. This was my lover, the man who cared for me and sometimes shared my bed. If I couldn't trust him, I could forget about any future that we might have together.

Taking a deep breath, I said, "Michael, I'm in trouble."

"Oh." His fingers loosened on my hand, and with an almost imperceptible movement, he shrank away.

*Shit! He thinks I'm pregnant.* The urge to confide died an instant death. I let him sweat for a minute before saying, "Did you read in the newspaper about George Pinkus, that

Toronto man murdered in the Atherton Arms last month?"

"I noticed the story. Didn't read it closely. Go on."

"He was somebody I knew from long ago. Until he got in touch with me a few weeks ago, I hadn't seen him for twenty years. He had my name in his address book. When the police found it, they questioned me. I admitted that I had visited George's hotel room just before he was killed."

"Why did you go there?"

My mouth was dry. I had to lick my lips before I could go on.

"To return his wallet. He had come over for coffee and accidentally left it here." I felt guilty, falling back upon this feeble lie. "Anyway, when I realized that I was a suspect, I went to Toronto to look up people who might have had a motive, because I didn't."

"You played detective?"

"Well, yes. The police gave no sign of being interested in anybody except me, yet I knew there must be many people who hated George Pinkus. One person whom I talked to lives in Rosedale."

"If the police suspect you," he said calmly, "they must think you have a motive."

"Blackmail. They think George was blackmailing me. It's crazy. But I suppose I have a bad enough reputation to make it believable."

"It's not that bad. To have an affair with a student was a mistake. But don't exaggerate."

He raised my hand to his lips and his eyes looked into mine. "Is there anything else you should tell me?"

"No," I murmured, looking away. I had said as much as I dared.

# Twenty

My transcription of the manuscript was not going well. It was not the secretary hand that caused me a problem. Nor was it the condition of the manuscript. Although there were places, chiefly at the outer edges of pages, where letters were blurred to illegibility, the context made clear what the word must be.

The real problem was physical. With its tight binding and old, brittle glue, the manuscript could not be opened fully. I could not lay it flat on my desk for copying. Ninety degrees was as wide as the pages could be spread. In order to read it, I had to hold my left thumb inside, holding the pages apart, with my fingers outside to steady the back.

Hunched over, my eyes only a few inches from the page, I soon got a cramp in my hand and a crick in my neck. My wrist stiffened. My shoulders ached. In a short time, the copying became a mechanical act, and I became a robot transcribing every letter, every punctuation mark, every line break in the blank verse.

Although I was copying the play word for word, I could not say that I was reading it. Coping with both physical discomfort and the need to be accurate, I paid so little attention to meaning that I might as well have been transcribing a document in Polish, Latvian or Hungarian – all foreign to me. The part of my mind that was actually thinking had other things to occupy it, such as the fact that George's killer was still out there and still did not have the manuscript.

For ten days nothing stopped my progress. I transcribed, I ate, I slept, and I tutored Sebastian. By the time I had copied the word "finis" after the closing couplet, my eyes itched, my head throbbed, and the words I had written were a blur. I riffled the pages of my copy: one hundred and sixty-four pages of lined paper in a three-ring binder.

I felt about ninety years old as I rose creakily from my chair. It was eleven p.m. *That's it,* I thought as I wrapped the manuscript and slid it into the waterproof pouch. Back to the refrigerator for *Cardenio.* For me, a warm bath and a long soak in the tub.

The next day, after Sebastian's tutorial, I sat down to read the play straight through from start to finish, the way a play needs to be read.

Before the end of the first act, I knew that something was wrong.

The surfeit of "sirs" in the opening speeches had already concerned me. It had struck me the very evening that George brought the manuscript to my home. Now I underlined every use of "sir" in Cardenio and Pedro's conversation:

> *Cardenio.* These seven days spent from home have now undone
> My peace forever.

*Pedro.* Good, be patient, sir.

*Cardenio.* She is my wife by contract before Heaven
And all the angels, sir.

*Pedro.* I do believe you;
But where's the remedy now? Luscinda's gone.
Fernando hath possession.

*Cardenio.* There's the torment!

*Pedro.* This day, being the first of your return,
Unluckily proves the first of her fastening.
Her father holds a good opinion of the bridegroom,
As he's fair spoken, sir, and wondrous rich –

*Cardenio.* There goes the devil in a sheepskin!

*Pedro.* With all speed
They clapped it up suddenly: I cannot think, sure,
That Luscinda over-loves him; though being married,
Perhaps, for her own credit, she doth intend
Performance of an honest, duteous wife.

*Cardenio.* Sir, in this sad business, question nothing.
You will but lose your labour; 'tis not fit
For any, hardly mine own secrecy,
To know what I intend. I take my leave, sir.
I find such strange employments in myself,
That unless death pity me and lay me down,
I shall not sleep these seven years, sir.

Six redundant "sirs", whose only function was to make up a ten-syllable line of iambic pentameter blank verse! How to explain it? Shakespeare could write iambic pentameters in his sleep – well, not literally – but he never needed to pad a line.

I rationalized: Shakespeare wrote *Cardenio* at the end of his career. He was about to retire, probably in poor health. The surfeit of sirs could be dismissed as a minor issue.

I wanted Shakespeare to be the author, wanted it so much that the desire clouded my judgment. Like a trusting wife who finds lipstick on her husband's collar, I tried to ignore unwelcome evidence.

But more lay ahead. The serious problems began with the wedding banquet.

Wedding banquet? What wedding banquet? In Cervantes' story, Luscinda faints, her mother finds a letter hidden in her bosom, the groom tries to stab the bride, and the marriage ceremony breaks up in disarray. This would have been great dramatic action. The audience would have loved it. But the playwright had not used it.

Instead, he served up a wedding banquet.

In the play, nothing disrupts the celebration. No fainting. No letter. No dagger. As one character observes:

> Here's marriage sweetly honoured in gorged
> stomachs
> And overflowing cups!

The cups continue to overflow until Luscinda's father proposes the final toast to the bride, "A health from a strange cup," he announces.

Strange, indeed, for the wine cup was formed from a human skull. The guests gasp. Luscinda's father goes on to say:

> My wife, I know, will pledge us, though the cup
> Was once her father's head ...

In an aside to the audience, Luscinda's mother expresses her outrage, as well she should.

This was a curious addition to the story. It made me pause, but I was ready to explain it away. Shakespeare often added subplots to the main action. Revenge stories were extremely popular in his day. It would be a bizarre twist for Luscinda's mother to seek vengeance upon her husband for her father's death, but no stranger than many complications that appear in Jacobean drama. I could accept that if I tried.

I read on, expecting Cardenio to reappear at any moment, raging madly in the mountains.

But in the play he does not go mad. When he makes his next appearance, he is perfectly sane. Instead of running off to the mountains, he has disguised himself as a servant employed in the Fernando/Luscinda household. His plan, as he explains to the audience, is to break up Fernando and Luscinda's marriage.

His first step must be to prevent its consummation. This is essential. The contemporary audience will expect the heroine to remain a virgin until the hero finally wins her back. Haste is necessary. The wedding banquet is already in progress. Before the newlyweds go to bed, Cardenio must procure a charm that will render Fernando sexually impotent.

In a scene reminiscent of Macbeth's visit to the three Weird Sisters, Cardenio seeks out the notorious witch Hecate. After a suitable amount of incantation, Hecate obligingly provides Cardenio with a charm made from serpents' skins woven together with special knots. She tells him:

So sure into what house these are conveyed,
Knit with these charms and retentive knots,
Neither the man begets nor woman breeds,
No, nor performs the least desires of wedlock,
Being then a mutual duty.

The charm is effective. Fernando appears the next morning bewailing his failure to fulfil his duty as a husband.

With Luscinda's virginity safeguarded, surely the time has come for Cardenio to head for the mountains! But for the next few scenes, there is no clue to his whereabouts. Hecate, her incestuous son Firestone, a coven of witches and a throng of demons have taken over the play.

By the time I had reached the end of Act One, I could deny no longer. The play wasn't right. Not right at all.

The plot wasn't right.

No. The characters weren't right.

No. It was more than that. Everything was wrong.

Yet I kept reading to the end.

Cardenio never does go mad or run away to the mountains. But Fernando meets with the fate he deserves, although by accident:

A fearful, unexpected accident, for Fernando
From a false trap-door fell into a depth
Exceeds a temple's height, which takes into it
Part of the dungeon that falls three-score fathom
Under the castle.

No repentance by the sinner. No forced marriage. No Dorotea. In fact, Fernando's forsaken sweetheart is missing from the play.

Luscinda's mother forgives her husband, who promises to give her father's skull a decent, Christian burial.

Luscinda, the virgin widow, is free to marry Cardenio and live happily ever after.

And in all times may this day ever prove
A day of triumph, joy, and honest love!

Enough! I put down my pen. Shakespeare did not write this play.

Staring at the closing lines, my chin resting on my hand, I cursed the unfairness of life. I felt drained, with nothing left in me but anger and disappointment. I blamed myself for my gullibility. I mourned the loss of my twenty-five thousand dollars. I fantasized about what I would do to George if he were not already dead.

Downstairs, the hall clock chimed eight. I closed the binder. For a minute I rested my head on the desk. Then I went down to the kitchen and made a cup of tea, which I carried out to the porch.

Rocking slowly in the swing, I listened to the jarring of the nighthawks as they swooped and dived over the rooftops. It was August now. Fireflies glimmered in the bushes in front of the house. The maple leaves in the glare under the streetlight held their green, but those fluttering above the metal shield were black in the grey-blue dusk. Daylight seeped from the sky, just as my hopes of fame and fortune had seeped away.

The manuscript for which George Pinkus had died was not Shakespeare's *Cardenio*.

# Twenty-one

Next morning, while my coffee brewed, I glanced through the morning paper. One particular story caught my eye. A young writer, a sophomore at an Ivy League university, had been caught plagiarizing. Her best-selling novel contained passages cribbed from another author's work. The publisher had recalled all copies and demanded the return of the advance on royalties. The offending book would vanish, and deservedly so. To pass off another's work as your own is theft, a deed as criminal as to write a bogus cheque.

I poured a mug of coffee and carried it out to the porch.

How could a day be so glorious when I was filled with gloom? The green trees were vivid against a cloudless blue sky. Shadows of leaves danced over the lawn.

Only the sad cooing of the mourning doves harmonized with my mood. I stared into my coffee mug and fantasized about what might have been. I felt like a loser, because that's what losers do: fantasize and feel sorry for themselves.

Maybe it was time to take a break from scholarship. To do what? Weed Professor Weaver's flowerbeds? Scrub the kitchen floor? Even to contemplate such chores sapped my energy. I wished I had brought the newspaper out to the swing. I could be reading about all the disasters in the rest of the world. Suicide bombers blowing people up in the

Middle East. Erupting volcanoes burying towns in lava and ash. Tsunamis wiping out cities.

I was considering how much effort it would take to walk back inside to get the newspaper when I noticed Sebastian loping toward the house, *Norton Anthology* in hand.

I glanced at my watch. Ten o'clock. The hour for his final tutorial had arrived, and I had completely forgotten about it.

He trotted up my front steps. Smiling. Eyes bright. What a reversal! Usually I was the enthusiastic partner in our enterprise.

I pulled my thoughts together, welcoming the distraction. Something like professional pride demanded that Sebastian do well. And after the hours invested in tutoring him, I had a personal interest in his success. It would be my success, as well.

After Sebastian and I had assured each other that it was a beautiful day, I asked, "Do you want to work outside while it's still cool?"

"Why not?" He dropped onto the swing beside me. Hastily I moved over to keep a space between us. Sebastian opened his book to the assigned poem, William Butler Yeats' "The Second Coming."

"Have you read it?" I asked.

"I glanced over it, more or less."

"All right. What does the title refer to?"

"The Second Coming? That's when Jesus is supposed to come back to earth, isn't it?"

"Right. Keep that in mind while you read the poem to me."

Bending his head over the book, Sebastian read:

Turning and turning in the widening gyre
The falcon cannot hear the falconer

He halted. "Deirdre, I've seen that."

"Really?"

"The falcon flies upward and out in circles that get wider and higher as it climbs." Sebastian swept his arm in circles through the air. "If it soars too far, the falconer can't summon it back." His eyes returned to the text. "What the devil does falconry have to do with Jesus?"

"Think of a cone," I said, my mind now engaged. "From the moment the falcon leaves the falconer's wrist, its flight traces the shape of a cone. For Yeats, images of cones diagram the cycles of history. The small point at the base is the dynamic event that begins a new cycle. For our present cycle, it was the birth of Jesus Christ."

Feeling the faint pressure of Sebastian's thigh, I shifted an inch further away. It was disconcerting to be sitting so close to him. He had a fresh, clean soapy smell. It crossed my mind that if I raised my fingers, I could touch the smooth skin of his throat and the wisps of blond hair that peeked above the open neck of his shirt. Focus! I told myself.

I cleared my throat. "From that starting point, the birth of Christ, the events of history spiralled up and out for two thousand years. Wider and higher until ... well, read on."

Sebastian read:

Things fall apart; the centre cannot hold;
Mere anarchy is loosed upon the world,
The blood-dimmed tide is loosed, and everywhere
The ceremony of innocence is drowned;

> The best lack all conviction, while the worst
> Are full of passionate intensity.

His eyebrows lifted. "Iraq? Afghanistan?"

"You got it. When I was your age we said, 'Vietnam.' Our parents said, 'Hitler.'"

Sebastian pointed to the date at the bottom of the poem. "1921. So it's a prophecy?"

"Yes. A prophecy based on a theory. Read the rest."

He read slowly, lingering over the final two lines:

> And what rough beast, its hour come round at last,
> Slouches towards Bethlehem to be born?

"Hm. Not much like Jesus." Sebastian frowned. "If that's how the next cycle begins, it sounds nasty. Do you think Yeats is right?"

"That's for you to decide. You're on your own."

"You think I'm ready?"

"As ready as you're going to be. When do you write?"

"One o'clock tomorrow." Sebastian closed his book.

I went into the house and brought out a copy of the previous year's final examination. Sebastian and I went over the questions until the two-hour lesson ended.

"Well, that's that." I said. "Give me a call afterwards, if you feel like discussing the exam."

Sebastian stood. "I'll drop over to see you."

"That won't be necessary. We can do a post-mortem over the phone."

"I'd rather come here."

"If you like."

When I wished him luck and shook his hand, he held onto mine a moment too long. I could have pulled my hand away. I didn't see why I should. For the past six weeks, I had been totally professional. But since I was no longer a member of faculty, I could let Sebastian hold my hand if I felt so inclined. A small indiscretion might cheer me up. As for Michael, he had made a major point that he did not belong to me, nor I to him.

The following afternoon, while Sebastian wrote his examination, I started typing the *Cardenio* text onto my hard drive. The day was hot and humid. Despite a small fan blowing air toward my face, I was wilting in the August heat.

My heart was not in my work. If Shakespeare did not write this play, how many people would give a damn who did? No appearance in the *New York Times* bestseller list. No interview with Oprah Winfrey.

In return for my twenty-five thousand dollars, I had on my hands a Seventeenth Century manuscript of unknown authorship that I might sell to a collector for five thousand ... on a good day. I might look it up on eBay. I might take it to *The Antiques Roadshow.*

If I had the morals of George Pinkus, I might try to invent evidence that it was Shakespeare's work. But even my elastic principles would not stretch that far. Besides, I'd never get away with it. Other scholars could smell a rat as well as I.

But where did the play come from? Who did write it? What was its title before the scam artist stole it?

If I managed to uncover the identity of the real author, my discovery could result in an interesting book that might help me to another university position. As far as profit went, I would be thinking thousands, not millions. But money isn't everything, I reminded myself as my mind began to rise to the challenge.

I turned off the computer, pushed back my chair from the desk, stood up and stretched. It was time to stop wallowing in self-pity. It was time for positive thinking. A cool drink might help. Down the stairs I went, pulled a bottle of iced tea from the fridge and carried it into the living room. I settled into the sofa, in the cool spot right under the ceiling fan.

From the far end of the room, the two tall bookcases flanking the fireplace faced me. The volumes on the shelves represented the works of every major Elizabethan and Jacobean dramatist. As I sipped my tea, I stared at the spines of all those books.

Where to begin?

Fraud wasn't invented yesterday. Scam artists have been with us since the Serpent fooled Eve in the Garden of Eden. Back in the Sixteen Hundreds, I reasoned, somebody had seen a golden opportunity to cash in on Shakespeare's growing fame. It had grown fast in the years immediately after his death. The *First Folio,* which Shakespeare's colleagues had brought out in 1623, was a huge success.

*Cardenio* was not among the included plays.

Why not?

Possibly the compilers of the *First Folio* could not find a manuscript from which to print it. That might well have been the case if the prompt copy had perished in the fire that destroyed the Globe Theatre in 1613. Or perhaps the compilers rejected *Cardenio,* as they rejected *Pericles,* as not entirely Shakespeare's work. Whatever the reason, they had not included *Cardenio.*

Enter the unscrupulous entrepreneur. I pictured him as a seventeenth-century George Pinkus, arrayed in a worn doublet, baggy hose, and a not-too-clean ruff. Noticing both the popularity of the *First Folio* and also the absence from it of *Cardenio,* he saw a chance to supply the lack.

What did he do? Unable to find a genuine manuscript of *Cardenio,* he looked around for an obscure play whose plot bore some resemblance. In all probability, he had seen the real *Cardenio* onstage. After finding a play that would do, he doctored it, changed characters' names, and copied it in the slightly old-fashioned secretary hand – the handwriting that Shakespeare used.

Finally, to authenticate the fraud, my scam artist (or his associate, for the handwriting had to be different) forged the licence granted by George Buck, the Master of the Revels.

To test this theory, I had to find that stolen play. The place to search was in the works of Shakespeare's contemporaries. I looked up at my crowded bookshelves. There they were: the dramas of Christopher Marlowe, George Chapman, Ben Jonson, John Webster, Thomas Middleton, and more. Without leaving the house, I might stumble upon the very play I was looking for.

Stumble upon was not good enough. I needed a plan.

Dates were the key. Interest in Shakespeare's plays surged when the *First Folio* appeared in 1623, remaining strong until the Puritans closed the theatres in 1642. With the theatres closed, there was no market for plays. The practising playwrights either retired or found other employment. With no money to be made from plays, there was no longer a motive for stealing another dramatist's work. This being the case, the fraud must have been committed within the intervening nineteen years.

There was one further limitation. The dramatist whose work was stolen had to be deceased at the time of the theft. Anyone who pirated the work of a living playwright would have risked a lawsuit, for Shakespeare and his contemporaries lived in a particularly litigious age. And so, I concluded, I was looking for the work of a dramatist already dead before 1642.

I went back upstairs to the study, turned on the computer, and made my list:

| | | |
|---|---|---|
| John Fletcher | d. 1625 | (possible collaborator on the real *Cardenio*) |
| Cyril Tourneur | d. 1626 | |
| William Rowley | d. 1626 | |
| Thomas Midddleton | d. 1627 | |
| Thomas Dekker | d. 1632 | |
| George Chapman | d. 1634 | |
| John Marston | d. 1634 | |
| Ben Jonson | d. 1637 | |
| John Webster | d. 1638 | |
| Shakerley Marmion | d. 1639 | |
| John Day | d. 1640 | |
| Philip Massinger | d. 1640 | |

Now this was progress! I nearly forgot about Sebastian's examination until, glancing at my watch, I saw that the time was close to three o'clock.

Sebastian should be two-thirds of the way through his exam, hunched at a desk in the gym, perhaps with his pen flying furiously over the page, or perhaps with his chin in his hands, stumped. He knew enough to pass, if only he could remember to back up his opinions with reference to the text. A Sebastian flight of fancy might cancel all our careful preparation. A quick prayer for his success was the most I could do for him now.

Turning off the computer, I returned to the living room to get started on my own project. I lifted Volume I of the *Works of John Fletcher* from its shelf.

Methodically, I began to make my way through the volume, though my thoughts were half with Sebastian as I read. When the hall clock struck four, I could virtually hear the chief invigilator's command: "Stop writing, please!"

As if in response to the command, I closed the book halfway through *The Scornful Lady.* There was time for a shower before Sebastian arrived.

I needed a shower. It was one of those days when the air feels like a saturated sponge. The noon-hour forecast had warned of evening thunderstorms.

# Twenty-two

By the time my doorbell rang at five, I was as nervous as if I were the one who had written the exam.

On opening the door, the first thing I saw was Sebastian's smile. The second was the LCBO bag he held out to me, with the shoulders and neck of a magnum of champagne looming over the top.

Sebastian looked fresh and clean. There was assurance in the way he held his head. He wore a crisp white shirt, open at the neck, and light beige slacks. Obviously, he had gone back to his hotel to change.

"*Dom Perignon* 1996," he said. "Already chilled." Beads of condensation covered the exposed shoulders and neck of the bottle. Perspiration glistened on Sebastian's forehead and upper lip.

I blinked. He must have paid a fortune for that vintage.

"So the exam went well?" I said.

"Brilliant."

Brilliant was more than I would bet on, yet such optimism suggested that he likely did pass.

"Then it's time to celebrate," I said. "We've earned the champagne."

Carrying the huge bottle, Sebastian followed me into the kitchen, where I found a tin of smoked oysters and a box of crackers in the cupboard. By the time he had untwisted the wires and popped the cork, I had arranged the oysters and crackers on a plate and located a pair of champagne flutes.

"This is the first time I've used these," I said as I rinsed the glasses under the tap. "I seldom have an occasion to drink champagne."

"Sweets to the sweet," he said.

"That's Gertrude's line," I objected.

He popped an oyster into his mouth. "Methinks the lady doth protest too much."

As I wiped the flutes with a tea towel, he stood at my shoulder. "I think I shall call you Gertrude," he said.

"If you do, you'd better stop stealing my lines."

We carried flutes, champagne and oysters into the living room. Sebastian poured. We clinked our glasses.

"To literature!" Sebastian said.

"And to your success," I replied, hoping that premature celebration wouldn't jinx his results.

We drank the first glass while standing. Sebastian poured a second. We clinked again.

"This is good stuff," I said. "The bubbles make my mouth tingle."

"Wait till it reaches your brain."

"Before that happens, you want to review the examination, don't you? Isn't that why you're here."

Sebastian smiled. "Righto!"

Setting his flute on the coffee table in front of the sofa, he pulled a folded paper from his slacks' pocket. He handed the paper to me.

"Let's see." I unfolded the paper and sat down on the sofa. Sebastian settled beside me. "Part A: Essay Questions. Five topics offered. You had to write on three."

"I chose Chaucer first," he said. "I wrote about the cross-section of society portrayed in the Prologue – all those different sorts of people setting off on a pilgrimage together."

While we drank a third glass of bubbly, he outlined the details of his answer. *Not bad,* I thought. *It sounds like a B+.*

Over our fourth glass, he analyzed the moral issues in *Hamlet,* which Sebastian seemed to have muddled slightly. That might be Shakespeare's fault. Or perhaps it was the effect of champagne upon Sebastian's powers of recollection. *C- . But still a pass.*

A fifth glass, while discussing "The Second Coming," brought us both to the conclusion that wisdom lay in forgetting about the future.

*"Carpe diem,"* I said. "Seize the day. Eat an oyster."

Carefully placing a smoked oyster upon a cracker, I popped it into my mouth. Then I fed an oyster to Sebastian – I'm not sure why, but it seemed a good idea. Through the next glass of champagne, we fed oysters to each other.

Noticing the examination paper, which was lying on the sofa between us, I recalled the purpose of Sebastian's visit. I picked up the paper.

"Shall we continue?" I asked.

"Oh, why bother? Do you think I earned an A?"

"Absolutely." I kissed Sebastian's cheek. "You're not so dumb."

"And you're not so old," he murmured as his fingers tugged the waistband of my skirt.

Old! That's the wrong word for a man to use when his hand is exploring under a woman's blouse. I briefly considered pushing his hand away. I might have, too, if his fingers had not found what they were looking for. When he started caressing my nipple, "Stop" turned into a moan of pleasure. His fingers continued stroking. I told myself, *What the hell! It isn't as if we haven't done this before.*

We half slid, half rolled from the sofa onto Professor Weaver's Persian carpet. I felt the soft pile under my bare butt and hung there for an instant, coldly conscious, lecturing myself that I'd be sorry. But it was too late to listen to reason. My body was pressed to his, and I was falling fast.

Afterwards, I raised myself on one elbow and stroked his face with my free hand. He opened his eyes, blinked, smiled, then closed his eyes again.

Distant thunder rumbled. The room darkened. I pulled myself up from the carpet and switched on a table lamp, then pulled a cushion from the sofa and placed it under his head. He lay on his back, with his face slightly tilted to one side. The blond stubble of his ridiculous buzz cut was golden against the crimson pillow. His long eyelashes lay like a baby's on his cheeks, and his lips were slightly parted in a pout. He is a boy, I thought, and he is not for me.

Our bodies had connected for old time's sake, and it would never happen again. Michael didn't have to know, although it did not matter if he did. We had settled the freedom question. My body belonged to me, not to him. But still it would be better if he didn't know. Men who believe in sexual freedom usually mean it only for themselves.

The hall clock chimed nine. The sound echoed in my head. I had a fuzzy thought that Sebastian should leave. My head ached, my stomach churned, and I felt weepy. We shouldn't have had sex. My weakness for Sebastian had already caused too many complications in my life.

I retrieved my panties and pulled them on. I smoothed my skirt, which I was still wearing. No brassiere. For half a minute I didn't know what had happened to my blouse. But then I found it mashed between two sofa cushions, struggled into it, and did up a couple of buttons. With my breasts covered, I felt more or less in control.

Gently I shook Sebastian's shoulder. "It's time for you to leave."

"Noooo," he groaned.

"Yes," I insisted. "You can't stay here all night. Consider my reputation."

I didn't expect immediate compliance. It took a minute or two before Sebastian sat up and pulled his fingers through his hair, then pressed them against his temples. Shakily he rose to his feet and staggered into the front hall.

"Where are you going?" I asked.

He grunted unintelligibly, half turned toward me before losing his balance. One shoulder smacked the front door. His hand grabbed the knob.

"Wait!" I cried out. "You can't go back to your hotel like that. You're naked. Put on your clothes."

He wagged his head hard, as if trying to clear it.

"I'm not leaving. Just going up to the loo." From the muffled thumps of his ascent, I think he went up the stairs on his hands and knees.

I waited for him to return. The toilet flushed. Then silence. He should be back soon. I got up from the sofa, picked up his briefs, slacks and shirt, folded them and placed them on a chair. What if he had passed out in the bathroom? I wondered whether he had locked the door.

At that moment, the champagne and oysters caught up with me. Too much champagne. Way, way too much. I barely made it to the kitchen sink before it all came up, leaving me with a throbbing head. Champagne never did agree with me, not to mention the smoked oysters.

I tottered back to the living room and lay down on the sofa to wait for the room to stop spinning. I felt as if I were in a small boat rocking in heavy seas. Sebastian might as well stay in the bathroom, handy to the toilet bowl, if he felt the way I did. I couldn't very well throw him out in that condition. We'd matched each other, glass for glass. I should have had more sense. Laying my aching head on a cushion, I closed my eyes.

Immediately I dropped into sleep – a troubled sleep in which a severed hand pawed at my breast. It was a relief when rolling thunder woke me up.

Lightning flashes lit up the room. Rain lashed the window glass. The gauzy drapes billowed and flapped like sails. I realized that I should close the windows but felt too tired and ill to move. I was cold too, but couldn't think what to do about that, beyond hugging myself and pressing my shivering body against the sofa cushions.

The clock chimed four. Simultaneously, I heard noises at the front door. A key turned in the lock. The bolt slid back. The floor creaked.

# Twenty-three

When a prowler enters, let him prowl. Let him take your jewellery, your cash, and your credit cards. Play possum. That's what everybody says to do. If the intruder thinks you are asleep, he won't need to kill you.

Outdoors, thunder growled and wind roared in the trees. Indoors, the clock ticked and the floor creaked. Huddled on the sofa, I held my breath as the prowler's footsteps crossed the hall, heading towards the staircase, not into the living room. He started up the stairs. Slowly. It was an old house. Every tread squeaked. At each step, he held a beat.

I strained to hear. A minute passed – so it seemed – before I heard his footsteps directly overhead. He was in my bedroom. In the middle of the night that's where I should have been, not here on the sofa, limp and sick from champagne. What would he have done if he had found me in my bed?

Now was my chance to get away. While the intruder was upstairs, I could make a break for the front door. The odds were good. But I could not move. Terror held me numb. Like a child who pulls the covers over his head to hide from the bogeyman, I pushed myself deep into the cushions.

The prowler left the bedroom. He was still upstairs, though I didn't know which room he was in.

Where was Sebastian? His clothes were still on the living-room chair. So he had not left the house. He must be upstairs too, maybe asleep on the bathroom floor. If the prowler encountered him, there would be a commotion. Even if the prowler killed him in his sleep, there would be some kind of noise. I listened for a shout, a thump, any kind of sound, and heard nothing but footsteps in the upstairs hall, approaching the top of the stairs.

Lightning flashed. With a clap of thunder, the street light and the table lamp went out.

The stairs creaked again. The prowler was coming down. Why couldn't I have run for it while I had the chance? Too late now. I was shivering, but not from cold. Too scared to be cold. My heart was hammering in my chest by the time he reached the bottom of the stairs. He entered the living room.

I heard harsh breathing, smelled sandalwood, saw a familiar silhouette against the gauze drapes. Mother of God! It couldn't be!

Lightning flooded the room. In the instant I saw Michael, he saw me. A split second later, we were in darkness again.

"Michael!" I sat up. "What are you doing here?"

Why would my lover come to me like a thief in the night? I could see only his shape in the darkness.

"How did you get in?" My voice shrilled. "I never gave you a key."

"I borrowed your spare house key, the one you keep on a hook by the back door, and I had it copied."

The beam of his flashlight suddenly struck my face. I could see nothing but the light shining straight into my eyes.

"You had my key copied?"

"That's right."

"When? Why?"

"I borrowed it from the hook the day we finished packing Professor Weaver's books."

"I can't believe this. Why would you copy the house key of a woman you'd just met?"

"Remember the Boy Scout motto? Be Prepared."

"Prepared for what?"

At that moment, after a preliminary flicker, the electricity surged on. By the table lamp's light I saw Michael's face, tight as a fist, and his brown hair matted with rain. He switched off his flashlight. It was one of those small ones, the size of a cake of soap. He put it in his pocket.

"You look like a drowned rat," I laughed shakily. "What's this all about? Were you trying to scare me? Check up on me?"

I swung my feet off the sofa and stood up. His eyes swept up and down my body. My hands flew to my half-unbuttoned blouse.

He saw the champagne glasses, the empty bottle, and the plate with its litter of cracker crumbs on the coffee table. But he did not appear to notice the neat pile of Sebastian's clothes on the chair.

"Had company, eh? Who was it? That British twit?"

"None of your business," I snapped. "Remember. I don't own you. You don't own me."

"It's not you that I'm after. I want the manuscript." He eyed me narrowly. "Where is it?"

I opened my mouth, and then closed it. He couldn't mean *Cardenio.* He didn't know about *Cardenio.*

With one swift motion he pulled something from the back of his pants. I heard a click. In his hand was a knife with a long, narrow blade. Not a Boy Scout knife. I took a step backward.

"What manuscript?"

"You know what I'm talking about. Don't play games."

*"Cardenio."* My voice was a whisper.

"When we were unpacking your books, you told me to watch out for your copy of *Don Quixote.* Of all the books in those boxes, why did you want to read *Don Quixote* at that particular time? Then later, why did you fly off the handle when I looked at the notes you were taking? I should have figured it out then, especially since Pinkus had mentioned that he knew you."

Michael stood in the doorway. It was a double doorway, never closed, with pocket doors hidden in the walls. He had blocked my escape route by planting himself there, but that suited me fine. With his back to the hall, he couldn't see anyone come down the stairs.

Play for time, I thought, keep him talking. Sebastian was upstairs. Michael didn't know that. Sooner or later, Sebastian would come down. Michael watched me. My eyes were on the knife. I took a step backwards.

"How did you know George Pinkus?" I asked.

"He contacted me about eighteen months ago. I was in Alberta, teaching at William Aberhart University. Pinkus told me he was looking for a buyer for an old manuscript he'd come upon. He said it might be Shakespeare's lost play. I was skeptical, until he mailed me a photocopy of the front page and the back page. Quite amazing. He was asking one hundred thousand dollars."

"Why did he think you'd be interested?"

"He ran across an article I'd written a dozen years ago. Before narrowing my field to literary criticism, I'd done some work on seventeenth-century texts."

"I didn't know that."

"There's a lot you didn't know."

Michael smirked. He was enjoying this. There's a certain exhilaration in telling secrets, even guilty secrets, especially when it provides an opportunity to display one's cleverness.

"Did you say he offered you the manuscript for one hundred thousand? No strings attached? Not a partnership?"

"Nothing so complicated. One simple transaction. I told him I'd let him know."

"And did you?"

"Not right away. I'd moved pretty well into criticism and wasn't sure I wanted to make a mid-career change. But I thought of the money to be made and eventually gave him a call. We came to terms. Of course I insisted on examining the manuscript before committing myself. I told him I was planning to go to Toronto for the Learned Societies' meetings a year ago last June. He said he could let me look at it then."

"The Learneds? I was there."

"Yes, I heard your lecture on *The Tempest,* but I didn't stay for the reception. I had arranged to meet Pinkus at the Royal York Hotel."

I backed a couple of steps toward the fireplace, where the fire irons stood in their stand. Brush. Shovel. Tongs. The poker with its spear-like point and its sharp hook – first cousin to the mediaeval halberd. I was calm now. Calm enough to consider a strategy.

"So George took the manuscript to the Royal York?"

"In a briefcase handcuffed to his wrist. We met in the lobby, and certainly received some curious glances when he fished out his keys and took off the handcuffs." Michael's mouth twisted in a grim smile. "When I made a quip about bracelets, he said he was afraid about somebody snatching the briefcase, like some old lady's purse."

As Michael spoke, the point of his knife sagged. He jerked it up. I took another step backwards. He advanced. The knife was steady in his hands. He aimed first at my throat, then just below my breastbone. The point dipped a fraction toward my stomach. Was he choosing a soft spot for the blade to enter?

"I'm not here to make conversation." His voice and his face tightened. "Let's get the manuscript."

Where was Sebastian? I was running out of things to say.

"Just a moment," I babbled. "While I was in Toronto, somebody entered this house. Was it you?"

"Yes, as a matter of fact."

"You know you let Socrates in?"

"The cat?" The corners of his mouth lifted. "Sneaky little brute!"

"But you didn't find anything, did you? I'd taken *Cardenio* with me to Toronto."

"That's what I figured. Either that, or I was on the wrong track. I still wasn't sure. But when you told me the police had you under investigation, I realized that you must have visited Pinkus' room before I did. And he gave the manuscript to you. Of course, I didn't know that at the time. When I took the briefcase, I assumed the manuscript was in it. It was a pleasant surprise to find twenty-five thousand dollars. But what I wanted was the manuscript. I still do."

He took a step toward me. I took a step back. My body shook from head to toe, and my tongue felt like it was stuck to the roof of my mouth. But I had to keep talking. I had to keep him talking. I was a dead woman if I could not.

"George tried to sell it to both of us," I said. "You first. Then he must have had second thoughts. He didn't offer it to me until after he arrived in Atherton."

"He came here to deliver it to me," Michael said. "The deal was, I'd deposit ten thousand dollars in his bank account as a down payment, then pay the rest in cash when he handed over the manuscript."

"He must have figured that he'd be better off to make a deal with me," I said. "I could pay him only twenty-five thousand. But as sleeping partner, Pinkus would receive income for life."

"The bastard already had my ten thousand. When I arrived at the Atherton Arms, he had that damn briefcase handcuffed to his wrist and was practically out the door. I was five minutes early. You should have seen his face when he saw me. White as a sheet." Michael laughed – a dry, mirthless sound, like a cough. "'Where do you think you're going?' I asked him. I assumed that he'd found a better deal with somebody else. I didn't know it was you."

"So you'd gone there with ninety thousand dollars to conclude the deal?"

"Don't be naïve. The ten thousand was all I intended to pay." His eyes shifted from me to the knife in his hand. "I figured the sight of this blade would persuade Pinkus to hand over the manuscript. I didn't plan to kill him. I knew he wouldn't go to the police. But as soon as he saw me put my hand in my pocket, he bolted for the door. I spotted a clock radio on the bedside table, yanked out the cord. Not a great weapon. But with one hand manacled to the briefcase, he couldn't defend himself."

"So you knocked him unconscious and cut off his hand."

"With this little gadget. Surgical steel. It took thirty seconds. Quicker than searching his pockets for keys." Michael laughed again. The same dry sound. "Now, Deirdre, you hand over the manuscript, or it's your turn."

"The joke is on you." I tried to force a laugh. "Whether you kill me or not, the manuscript is a fake."

For a split second I saw doubt in his eyes. Then his face hardened.

"Nonsense. I've seen it. Nobody could fake a thing like that. It's four centuries old if it's a day."

"But it's not Shakespeare's *Cardenio.* You killed George Pinkus for a four-hundred-year-old fraud."

"Shut up, Deirdre. You're getting hysterical."

Not a bad idea. Maybe I should start screaming. That should bring Sebastian on the double ... unless Michael reacted by driving that slender blade through my heart.

Two steps backward. My feet were on the hearthstones. My skirt brushed the fire tools stand. One more step. I reached my right hand behind my back, felt the hard metal knob at the top of the poker. If Michael turned around, I could grab it.

"George had it coming," I pleaded. "He screwed us both. We should talk about this. You and I could be partners."

"I don't need a partner. Come on, Deirdre. Get the manuscript."

There wasn't one foot of space between us. I could smell his sweat. I could hear my own heavy, ragged breathing and the loud ticking of the clock in the hall.

He flicked the knife between my collarbones. I felt blood trickle down my skin and between my breasts. Hardly any pain.

"I can slit your throat and look for the manuscript later," he said. "You might as well tell me where it is."

God! What could I do now? Now that he had confessed, Michael was going to kill me anyway. Maybe I should tell him. Every second I stayed alive increased the chance that Sebastian would come downstairs. Where the hell was he? Still in the bathroom?

"It's in the fridge."

He laughed. "So you finally found a use for your refrigerator – beyond making ice cubes. Now isn't that a clever hiding place!" He motioned with the knife. "Go ahead. I'll be right behind."

But I didn't move. Over Michael's shoulder I saw Sebastian coming down the staircase. A tread squeaked. Michael whirled around.

In an instant, I had the poker in my hands. I don't know where the strength came from as I raised that poker like a battle-axe and swung at his head. When it struck, the crunch of bone shivered up my arms. The hook disappeared in Michael's ear, right up to the shaft. The knife tumbled from his hand onto the carpet.

As Michael collapsed, I stumbled forward, still gripping the poker.

When I pulled out the hook, a splatter of blood cast crimson coins on the carpet. Michael on his knees, screaming, held his hand over his ear.

My legs buckled, and I collapsed on the chair beside the fireplace.

Sebastian had not moved. There he stood, halfway down the stairs, naked, his mouth agape. I waited for the trembling of my body to pass.

"Sebastian," I said. "Call nine-one-one. Ask for the police and an ambulance. And then get dressed."

# Twenty-four

Lights flashing and siren blaring, the EMS ambulance wheeled away from the curb, turned at the corner, and gathered speed as it wailed its way toward Atherton General Hospital.

I let the edge of the drape fall as I turned away from the window to face Police Detective Robert Agnew, who sat stiffly in the same leather armchair he had occupied the first time he questioned me. Constable Montour, copper-skinned and blue uniformed, black hair knotted in a bun at the back of her neck, perched, with her pen poised, on the chair she had carried in from the dining room. Sebastian stood with his back to the bookshelves, looking calm.

The table lamp was still lit, though sunshine filtering through the gauzy drapes gave ample light. Earlier, while the paramedics were strapping Michael to the stretcher and bandaging his streaming ear, neither Sebastian nor I nor Constable Montour had said a word. Detective Agnew had growled orders. Now, as the wail of the ambulance receded, no one spoke.

"Will he live?" I asked the silence around me.

"We have to wait for the doctor's report," Agnew said.

The living room had a slightly metallic, meaty smell. Professor Weaver's valuable Persian carpet was soaked with blood. A sprinkling of dark red droplets freckled the beige wall that was closest to where Michael had been standing. Amidst the carnage, only the knife was clean. It had bounced onto a clear space where it lay, the narrow blade shiny and bright. I pointed to it.

"That's the knife Michael used on George," I said. "He told me."

"The forensic team will be here soon," Agnew said. "Forensics can run tests. If that knife was used earlier to sever Pinkus' hand, there may be microscopic traces of tissue and blood." He looked from me to Sebastian. "Neither of you touched the knife, I hope."

"No." Sebastian and I spoke nearly in unison. I added, "Any fingerprints will be Michael's."

"Dr. Gunn, you had us fooled," Agnew said. "When we examined Pinkus' address book and saw your name and Michael Burton's, at first we thought all three of you were mixed up in some scheme together."

I caught my breath. "You mean the second name was Michael's? I certainly wish you'd told me sooner. Not knowing damn near got me killed."

"We were keeping an eye on Burton, but all the evidence pointed to you. Pinkus visited you, not Burton. Maybe we could have put a bug on Burton's phone, but he'd done nothing to arouse suspicion – except have his name in the address book. Besides, the hotel clerk identified you as the person who visited Pinkus' room two hours before he was found murdered. If Dr. Burton entered that room, he did it without being seen."

"If?" I demanded.

But why should Agnew take my word for it? Forensics still had to check the knife. The police had to complete their investigation before laying charges.

I glanced in Sebastian's direction, and he caught my gaze. Almost imperceptibly, he lifted one eyebrow. The look he gave me was grave, yet reassuring. Sebastian had taken charge.

Agnew continued, "When we saw you cozying up to Dr. Burton, we figured the two of you were working on something together."

"But we weren't," I said. "However it looked to you, our relationship was entirely personal – at least I saw it that way." I paused, thinking it over. Hadn't I sensed at the beginning that Michael was after something? O my prophetic soul! How was I to know that neither Professor Weaver's books, nor his house, nor my body had been what he was after?

Agnew turned to Sebastian. "Now, how do you fit into all this?"

"Dr. Gunn was kind enough to tutor me for an examination that I sat yesterday. To thank her, I brought a magnum of champagne, which we enjoyed together."

Agnew glanced at the empty glasses, the *Dom Perignon* magnum, and the plate with its cracker crumbs.

"You got drunk?"

"Actually, yes. I spent the night on the bathroom floor. On waking, I intended to call a taxi to take me to my hotel. When I opened the bathroom door, I heard voices from the living room. A man's voice and Dr. Gunn's. She sounded frightened. Not knowing what was going on, I started downstairs.

When I was halfway down, I could see the man she was talking to, but his back was to me. Dr. Gunn was facing me. I heard him say, 'Go ahead. I'll be right behind.' At the sound of my footsteps on the staircase, he turned, and I saw that he was holding a knife. Clearly, my appearance startled him. Dr. Gunn seized the chance to defend herself."

How discreet! How clearly expressed! Sebastian, you make me proud!

"Is that correct?" Agnew asked me. "Was Burton unaware of another person's presence in the house?"

"That's right. If I had told him, he might have killed me right away and then gone after Sebastian. Or he might have killed me and left Sebastian to take the blame. Think about it. What would have happened if Sebastian had come downstairs and found me with my throat slit and the living room awash in blood?"

Agnew nodded. "It would have looked bad for him."

Not great for me either. I could imagine what the media would have made of it. The notorious Dr. Gunn and her two lovers. Crime of passion. Well, I wouldn't have to worry about my future if I were dead.

Constable Montour looked up bright-eyed from her notebook. She was young, and probably found this case more interesting than most. It surely held enough intrigue to capture her attention.

Agnew resumed his questioning. "Do you know what motive Burton had? Was it jealousy? Or was it that manuscript you told us about?"

Constable Montour's pen started flying again.

"The manuscript. He killed George Pinkus to get it, and he was prepared to kill me."

"You still have the manuscript?"

"Yes."

"You'll have to hand it over to us."

I shrugged. "No objection. It's a fake anyway."

"That's not what you told Inspector Boothby when we questioned you at the station."

"I've had a chance to study it since then."

Outside, a car door slammed. I looked out the window. A police van had parked at the curb.

"That's forensics," Detective Agnew said. He glanced at Sebastian and me. "You two have to clear out."

"May we leave the premises?"

"It's up to you. We just don't want you hanging around the crime scene while the forensic team does its work."

I turned to Sebastian. "There's a Tim Hortons four blocks from here, on Main Street."

"Fine. We can both use a coffee."

Not knowing how much alcohol might still be in my system, I thought I'd better not drive. Sebastian and I walked. The morning breeze helped to clear my head.

"What are we going to do?" Sebastian asked after we had picked up our order and sat at one of the tables.

"I don't think that we have to do anything. Just wait."

Neither of us said much more. After a doughnut and coffee, I felt sufficiently restored to face whatever the rest of the day might hold. Sebastian hopped a bus to the Atherton Arms while I returned to Inchbury Street.

Back at the house, I found the forensic team packing the van with their gear and the collected evidence, which included the poker and the knife. I pointed at the blood-soaked carpet still lying on the floor. "What about that?" I asked Agnew.

"The photographer took plenty of pictures. You can have the carpet cleaned."

Detective Agnew was ready to leave.

"What about the poker?" I said.

"Eventually it will be returned. After the trial."

I thought about the courtroom dramas I had seen on TV. Exhibit A: the poker. Exhibit B: the knife. My mind leapt to an image of me on the witness stand and Michael in the prisoner's box.

"Any report on Michael's condition?"

"Serious but stable." He moved toward the door, opened it for Constable Montour. "I'll be in touch," he said. "Other charges may be pending."

"Against Michael?"

"I meant against you." His eyes narrowed. "Obstruction of Justice is a criminal offence."

He left before I could think of a response. Agnew was bound and determined to pin something on me, I figured. I'd have to get a lawyer. But first there was this other mess to clean up.

Alone in the living room, I contemplated the blood-soaked carpet, the splattered drapes and the speckled walls. I wondered about the best way to remove bloodstains from oak flooring and leather upholstery. Likely soap and water, if I acted fast. The sofa was brown leather, old and scuffed. Maybe a less than perfect job would do.

But before starting to clean anything, I e-mailed Professor Weaver. This had to be done, and quickly – before word from some other source caused him to question my suitability as a house-sitter. I began with an apology for sending bad news, and then offered a partial explanation of what had happened. Skirting the truth slightly, I tried to portray myself as the innocent victim of a home invasion. I concluded my message with a promise that everything would be made as good as new at my expense. With a bit of luck, Professor Weaver might never learn the details of what really happened.

How much would the cleaning cost? After turning off the computer, I sat for a moment at my desk, wondering if there were any way I could get my twenty-five thousand dollars back.

My fingers touched the small gauze bandage on my throat. Maybe I should have gone to Emergency for a couple of stitches. There would be a scar, but nothing disfiguring. It would be white and shiny, the size and shape of a freshwater pearl. A souvenir.

Suddenly the hall clock chimed, jerking me back to reality. Ten o'clock. Ken Hains would be opening his bookstore. He was the other person I wanted to phone. I had a question to ask my old friend, and I needed an answer.

I found his phone number in my address book. Ken answered on the second ring.

"Ken's Den, home of quality second-hand books."

"Hi, Ken. It's Deirdre."

"Hey. You weren't supposed to phone." His voice was shrill, nervous. "I asked you not to contact me."

"Relax. There's been an arrest."

"Really?" I heard the sharp intake of his breath, the slow exhalation. "Who?"

"The professor that Melrose hired to take my place in the English Department, Michael Burton. First-degree murder. I'm off the hook. So are you."

"That's a relief."

"Right." I paused. "But I have a question to ask you."

"Okay. What do you want to know?"

"Why you lied to me."

"Uh, about what, Deirdre?"

"You said you'd never been to Atherton."

"Oh."

"When you were looking for a pencil to write down my e-mail address, I picked up a pen from the floor. A red pen, with advertising. 'Bide your Time Budget Motel/Atherton, Ontario.'"

"I don't know where that pen came from. It doesn't mean –"

"That you stayed there. Maybe not. But I drove out to the motel and managed to check the guest register. Ken, you stayed there the night before George was murdered."

"I can explain."

"Go ahead."

"Remember, I told you that George tried to sell me an old manuscript."

"I do. And you told him you weren't interested."

"Right. But I had second thoughts. So I called him on his cellphone and made an offer, but he turned it down. He said he was in Atherton on business, and he told me where I could find him if I wanted to sweeten my offer. Something in his voice made me figure I had a chance. So I drove to Atherton and checked into that motel about eleven at night. When I tried to phone George, he was taking another call."

"That was probably me," I said. "We were haggling over the same manuscript."

"Christ! How many people did he string along?"

"At least three. But go on."

"I told him I was interested, but my top price was $20,000. He said, 'Forget it.' That made me furious, because I had driven all the way from Toronto. After we rang off, I went to bed. In the morning I checked out of my motel and drove around Atherton, looking over the Melrose campus. Remember, I hadn't been there before. Around noon, I thought I'd drop in at the Atherton Arms."

"Why?"

"I thought he might still be there. Maybe he still had the manuscript. If so, he might reconsider. George had told me his room number so I wouldn't have to ask for him at the desk. I stopped in the bar for lunch, then went up to his room."

"Did the desk clerk see you?"

"I didn't have to pass the desk. There was an exit from the bar to the rear of the lobby. I went up the staircase to the third floor. I found George's room. I knocked. No answer. I tried the doorknob. Then I called, 'Hey, George. It's me. Ken Hains.' I stood there, thinking he must have left. Then I saw the blood that had seeped under the door. It was dark and sticky, soaking the carpet. The toes of my shoes were in it. I pulled back. No way I was going to stick around. So I drove back to Toronto. Fast.

"When I reached home, I threw out my shoes and shampooed my car's floor mat on the driver's side. I figured I was in the clear. Then suddenly I remembered that I had touched the doorknob. My fingerprints were sure to be on it. The police didn't have my fingerprints on record. But if they knew I'd been in Atherton, I'd be in big trouble."

"So that's why you wrote me not to phone or e-mail."

"Either could have linked me to Atherton. Worse, it would have shown a connection to somebody already under suspicion. So that's why I warned you off."

"It sounds as if your first thought was to save your own skin." I slammed down the phone. So much for friendship!

# Twenty-five

**"SEX AND INTRIGUE AT MELROSE"**
**"MURDER IN THE GROVES OF ACADEME"**

The tabloids had a field day. Headline frenzy gripped even the staid *Atherton Advocate.* And the speculation! What was Dr. Gunn's student [and former lover] doing in her home at 4:00 a.m.? Why had Professor Michael Burton broken in? Who was George Pinkus? Another lover? The entanglements seemed without end.

My phone rang constantly with requests for interviews. Journalists pounded on my door. Paparazzi in the shrubbery aimed their cameras between gaps in the drapes.

Dr. Ian McBroom, Dean of Studies, issued a statement. "Recent regrettable incidents involving past and present faculty have in no way affected the reputation of Melrose University." Was he kidding?

The furor lasted for only one week. By then, something new had captured the attention of the media. Once again I could sit on the porch swing without cameras pointing at me, although cars driving along Inchbury Street continued to slow down as they passed the house. Sometimes people waved.

Hiding indoors during the week of media frenzy, I spent most of my time searching for the play that the plagiarist had doctored to create the false *Cardenio.* I had progressed through George Chapman and John Day and had nearly finished Thomas Dekker, when the final play in Volume III of Dekker's works caught my eye. *The Witch of Edmonton.* Could the witch be Hecate? If so, I might be on to something. Eagerly I turned to it.

> The Town of Edmonton hath lent the Stage
> A Devil and a Witch, both in an age.
> To make comparison it were uncivil,
> Between so even a pair, a Witch and Devil.

Alas! The Witch of Edmonton turned out to be a poor old crone named Mother Sawyer. There was no Hecate in Edmonton. After thumbing through the remainder of the text, I closed the book and carried Dekker back to the living room.

I was standing in front of the bookshelves, considering whether to start on the plays of John Fletcher before or after lunch, when I glanced out the living room window and noticed a taxi approaching along Inchbury Street. It stopped in front of the house. Not another reporter! I retreated from the window.

But no. It was Sebastian who stepped out onto the curb. He leaned in the cab window to pay the driver before turning toward the house. I had the front door open by the time the taxi pulled away. After days of turning pages, I was glad to see a friend.

"Good morning," he said. There was unusual vigour in his stride as he came up the front walk. From the bottom of the steps he looked up at me, holding out a bunch of long-stemmed red roses.

"For you." He trotted up the steps and thrust the flowers into my hands. Before I could thank him, he continued. "I have something important to tell you."

"The exam results? Already?"

"No. Not that."

"Did you win the lottery?"

"Not that either."

His eyes were bright with elation. Yet his mouth was twisted into the smile of someone embarrassed about his own good fortune.

"I must return to England."

"Really? I thought you couldn't."

"My father has died."

"I'm sorry."

"Please. No need for sympathy. Neither for him nor for me. He died of cancer that went into his bones. He'd been ill for two years. The family, at his insistence, kept it from me."

"Only to spare you," I said gently.

"Spare me? Oh, no. You didn't know my father. Stiff upper lip. Never show weakness, especially not to his useless son."

I sat down on the swing. When he joined me, I placed my hand on his. Poor Sebastian. The Prodigal Son must feel something to lose his father without a chance to ask forgiveness.

But no, Sebastian would never have asked forgiveness. Stubborn pride. He came by it honestly.

"I'm Sir Sebastian now." He spoke the words with a solemnity that struck me as absurd, as if he were about to be anointed with holy oil.

"Must I call you Sir?" I tried to joke.

"I don't expect it of a Colonial." He smiled, and the *gravitas* cracked. "But you may curtsey when we meet."

"I'll think about it."

My laughter fell upon silence.

"It isn't just a title," he said. "I own a village, a manor house, several hotels, and a diamond mine in South Africa. That's a good deal of responsibility for a chap who's barely twenty-four."

"I thought you were twenty-two."

"Time passes."

For a moment I said nothing, thinking how suddenly life can change. That's why people buy lottery tickets, isn't it? But for Sebastian there was no need. His destiny was handed to him whole on the day that he was born.

"When do you leave for England?" I asked.

"I have a seat on tonight's 8:00 p.m. flight from Toronto." His eyes were on a grey squirrel that was running across the lawn with a horse chestnut in its jaws.

I squeezed his hand. "Thanks for coming to tell me in person. I'd offer champagne if I had any." I forced a laugh. "But we've both had enough of that." I felt a lump in my throat; someone important was passing from my life.

"Offer me coffee. Then, if you have time, a lift to the university. There's business I want to attend to before I leave."

Of course he meant arrangements for the Registrar's Office to forward his exam results, and I was touched. For any practical purpose, it no longer mattered whether Sebastian passed English 201. But if he cared about his final mark, it meant that my tutoring and the literature we had read together had value in his eyes.

"Fine. I'll make a fresh pot."

For a few moments I didn't budge. Sebastian and I sat shoulder to shoulder, our fingers linked. I took my hand away and wiped it across my eyes.

"I better make the coffee," I said. I carried Sebastian's roses into the house to put them in water at the same time.

Minutes later, when I had brought out two steaming mugs, Sebastian said, "What about you?"

"My future plans?"

"Yes."

"Uncertain at present." Studiously sipping my coffee, I volunteered no further information.

"You lost your position because of me."

"No point bringing that up. I have other ways to make a living. And I'm doing research for a book."

"What sort of book?"

"I'm not sure. It might be a scholarly mystery, if such a genre exists. The subject will be a play called *Cardenio*."

"Never heard of it."

"Few people have." I set down my mug. "I had hoped it might be a lost play by Shakespeare. But it's not. It's somebody else's play, in disguise."

"The wolf in Bard's clothing?"

I allowed a smile. "That sums it up. My theory is, somebody four hundred years ago took an obscure play, doctored the text, and tried to pass it off as Shakespeare's lost play."

"Who was the real author?" Sebastian certainly was persistent. With so much on his own mind, why was he asking me these questions?

"I don't know, but I intend to find out."

"And then you'll write your book?"

"That will be the starting point. The real work doesn't begin until after I discover the identity of the person who actually wrote the play. There are dozens of unanswered questions about what was going on in the theatre in those years before the Puritans shut everything down in 1642."

"You must let me know when your book is published."

"That won't happen for two or three years, maybe more."

"So you'll receive no income from it for quite a while?"

"I'll manage," I said, somewhat curtly. My finances were not a subject that I wished to discuss. I stood up. "Isn't it time I gave you a lift to Melrose?"

While we were driving to the university, I said: "You'll have to come back for the trial, won't you?"

"That won't be for a few months."

"At least a few," I said.

I stopped the car in front of the Administration Building. "I could wait for you. We might have lunch."

He turned his lovely grey eyes on me.

"Sorry. But I must pack, and then catch the train to Toronto. Bit of a rush, unfortunately." He looked away, wrapped in his own thoughts.

I watched him stride up the broad concrete walk to the entrance and hold open the door for a blond girl in tight jeans, before he disappeared inside.

For a week I had been reading old Jacobean plays six hours every day, ploughing my way through the dramatists whose works were on my bookshelves.

It was difficult to stay focussed. Turning page after page was boring, and money worries distracted me even more. Even if I recovered my twenty-five thousand dollars, finances would still be tight. The confidence I had displayed to Sebastian was largely bravado.

Fortunately, I still had free housing. Professor Weaver had answered my e-mail with an assurance of complete faith in my dependability as a house-sitter. But there would be bills for gas, electricity and water, to say nothing of food.

The end of summer was near. Students were arriving in town, awakening Atherton from its long nap.

When Fall Term began, who would be teaching Michael Burton's classes? The English Department was short one instructor. To take care of English 202 and the undergraduate Shakespeare course, the administration could simply increase class sizes across the teaching loads of other professors. But to land someone qualified to conduct the post-graduate course in Textual Criticism? Fat chance!

Cancellation was not an option. In its calendar, the School of Graduate Studies had listed Textual Criticism as a course offering. By now, there must be students registered to take it. Fellowships had been awarded. Fees had been paid.

I knew that Melrose University needed me. I also knew that the Dean of Studies would rather have his fingernails pulled out than invite me back. But I could not help jumping every time the telephone rang.

The plays of Thomas Middleton, in two fat volumes, now rested on the kitchen table, where I was working to save the effort of lugging heavy books upstairs to the study. I did not expect to find the mystery play amongst Middleton's works. He was not obscure enough. The best known of his plays, *The Changeling*, still received occasional performance. But, wanting to be thorough, I had waded through Volume One and was skimming the Table of Contents of the second volume when an unfamiliar title caught my eye: *The Witch*. Hecate again? I turned straight to that play. And there it was:

ACT THE FIRST
SCENE I

An apartment in the House of the Lord Governor.
A banquet set out.

Enter Sebastian, Fernando.

*Seb.* My three years spent in war hath now undone
My peace for ever.

*Fer.* Good, be patient, sir.

*Seb.* She is my wife by contract before Heaven
And all the angels, sir.

*Fer.* I do believe you;
But where's the remedy now? You see she's gone,
Another hath possession.

*Seb.* There's the torment!

*Fer.* This day, being the first of your return,
Unluckily proves the first too of her fastening.

I felt like shouting, *Eureka!*

Without missing a metric beat, the original, "Three years spent in war," had become "Seven days spent from home." The plagiarist had given Middleton's Sebastian the name of Cardenio, Isabella the name of Luscinda, Antonio the name of Fernando, and Fernando the name of Pedro. Only Hecate had retained her original name. Now I knew why the witch played such a disproportionate role in the false *Cardenio*. In the play as Middleton wrote it, hers was the title role.

Reading through *The Witch*, I saw how little the plagiarist had needed to change. Apart from characters' names, pages and pages of dialogue and stage directions were exactly the same.

After reaching the "finis" of Middleton's play, I turned to the editor's notes. From them I learned that *The Witch* had remained unpublished during Middleton's lifetime and for one hundred and fifty-one years after his death. Not until 1778 was an edition printed from the only manuscript copy known to exist. And that single, unique copy was preserved in the Bodleian Library at Oxford University, where, if I only had the airfare, I could see it for myself.

Now what? Playing literary detective, I had solved the first half of the mystery. But – to use the language of crime fiction – I still did not know "Who done it." Nor did I anticipate that I could ever learn the name of the man behind the fraud. People like him – people like George Pinkus – leave no imprint on the world.

# Twenty-six

Michael was recovering, under police guard, at the Atherton General Hospital. The poker had nicked his carotid artery and blown apart the tiny bones deep in his right ear. The result would be permanent hearing loss. He faced two charges: First-degree Murder and Assault with a Deadly Weapon.

I was no longer a suspect. My life was no longer threatened. The police had recovered my twenty-five thousand dollars, having found the bundled banknotes in Michael's desk. There was a good chance that I could get my money back.

Looking at my situation objectively, I told myself that I had plenty to be thankful for. And yet my emotions were in turmoil. Anger. Isolation. Despair.

I remembered how Michael had helped to unpack my books. I remembered his head on my pillow. I remembered the knife.

A few times before, I'd been wrong about men, but never like this. There were days when I was ready to follow Cardenio's example – flee to the mountains and go mad. But there would be no Don Quixote to come to my rescue. Nobody's Dulcinea. That was me.

A knight in rusty armour would have done me no good. Not even a knight in shining armour. My rescuer turned out to be a lawyer. Smart, practical and thoroughly up-to-date, Miranda Cohen was a partner in Atherton's largest law firm, the prestigious Smith, Greenwood, McPhee, O'Connell and Cohen.

I met her by walking in the front door of the firm's handsome limestone building, a converted mansion on Court Street, and asking the receptionist if I could speak to a lawyer. Ms. Cohen was available.

She was in her late thirties, a dark-eyed, slim woman with silky brown hair and understated makeup, hardly more than a blush of peach on her full lips. She wore a beautifully tailored, pale grey linen suit, and took notes on creamy vellum with a gold-tipped fountain pen.

Before entering the law firm's offices, I had prepared an outline of events, starting with George Pinkus' arrival at my office and ending with Agnew's threat that the police might charge me with Obstruction of Justice. While I recited this litany, Ms. Cohen did not interrupt, keeping her eyes fixed upon me except to take down an occasional note.

"First," she said when I had finished, "I can ease your mind on one point. The charge of Obstruction of Justice will not stand. You were less than co-operative, no doubt. But you did nothing to protect the alleged killer or deliberately lead the police investigation in the wrong direction. As to the rest, let us consider how we shall proceed."

*"We,"* she had said. I brightened. Ms. Cohen was in my corner. I had a champion at last.

"I want you to recover my twenty-five thousand dollars," I said, "and restore the *Cardenio* manuscript to King's College if that is where it came from. George Pinkus' story about stealing it from the library stacks is plausible. But the university archivist should check. There might be a record of purchase or gift."

"I understand that when you acquired the manuscript, your intention was to return it eventually to the rightful owner?" Her level gaze dared me to say otherwise.

"Well, yes. Of course."

She nodded. "Good intentions can be important in a case like this. The fact is: you were in possession of stolen property. As an educated person, you know what that means. But we should be able to work things out. I'll get in touch with King's College." She paused. "Where is the manuscript now?"

"The police seized it."

"I'll make application to the Court to release it to King's College. Once the manuscript has been returned to its rightful owner, there's a good chance that you can recover the money expended to acquire it." She made another note, then looked up. "There's one more thing we must deal with: Melrose University's decision to deny you tenure."

"What about it?"

"Completely unjustified. The student you were involved with was not enrolled in a class that you taught. There was no abuse of authority. There was no harassment."

"Dr. McBroom, the Dean of Studies, acknowledged all that. Poor judgment displayed in my private life was the only reason given for the Senate's refusal to offer me tenure. And since the granting of tenure is in their sole discretion –"

"Nonsense! What if their sole discretion told them not to grant tenure to homosexuals? Or Blacks? Or Jews? In my opinion, Dr. Gunn, you have a cause of action."

"Are you saying that I should sue the university?" A wave of mingled hope and horror swept through me. I longed for tenure. On the other hand, a cash settlement might support me through the three years I needed to research and write my book. But litigation! Professors don't sue universities. It's not done.

"Don't look so shocked. One phone call to Dr. McBroom should get the ball rolling." The golden nib of Ms. Cohen's pen moved across the vellum. She looked up. "Normally, I would ask for a retainer. But I'll waive it this time and deduct my fee from the funds. Is that agreeable to you?"

A week passed, with no word from Ms. Cohen or from Melrose. I was becoming nervous. Should I phone Ms. Cohen? Should I phone the university? *Don't panic,* I told myself. *These things take time.* But we were running out of time.

Seven days before the start of Fall Term, the call came.

"Good morning," a man's deep voice said in answer to my hello, "Am I speaking to Dr. Gunn?"

That chilly, supercilious tone was unmistakable. Dr. McBroom was calling me. Not his secretary. The great man himself.

Steadying my voice, I replied. "It is."

"This is Ian McBroom."

"Ah, yes. How may I help you?"

"Dr. Gunn ..." He cleared his throat. "There is an important matter that we need to discuss."

My heart raced.

"Indeed?" I said calmly. "What might that be?"

"The subject is inappropriate for discussion over the telephone. Could you come to my office?"

"When do you suggest?"

"If possible, within the next forty-eight hours."

"I'll check my calendar."

*Stay cool,* I told myself. *He is the supplicant. Now I have the upper hand.* I took a few deep breaths. "I could be free the day after tomorrow at 11:00."

"I'll look forward to seeing you then." From the ice in his voice, I doubted whether he took much pleasure in the prospect.

Carefully, I set down the receiver. So the wheels were turning. What else had Ms. Cohen achieved on my behalf? It was time to ask for a progress report. Ms. Cohen's business card stared at me from the refrigerator door. I punched in her number.

"Ms. Cohen is in court this morning," her secretary said. "However, she was planning to phone you as soon as she returned to the office. She asked me to fit you in tomorrow morning. Will 9:45 be convenient?"

"I'll be there," I said.

When I arrived the next morning at the offices of Smith, Greenwood, McPhee, O'Connell and Cohen, Ms. Cohen was wearing a tailored, pearl-grey dress with gold accessories.

Understated, but smart. I wished that I had worn my Holt Renfrew suit instead of the white blouse and black skirt that had seemed appropriate when I pulled them out of the closet.

After an exchange of pleasantries, I got to the point. "Dr. McBroom phoned me yesterday."

"I'm not surprised. When I called him, I mentioned the possibility of a lawsuit."

"How did he react?"

"He became belligerent. That's a common reaction. The threat of litigation takes time to sink in. Once it does, the reasonable response is to avoid it at all costs." She leaned back in her chair. "What did he say?"

"He wanted a meeting to discuss what he calls an important matter."

"When?"

"Tomorrow morning."

"Excellent. Let me know what transpires." With a smile, she rose from her desk. "Now I have something for you." She bent to open a small metal safe mounted into the wall. After a few clicks, the door opened. I watched, mesmerized, as Ms. Cohen carried to her desk twenty-five neat packets of fifty-dollar bills. "The court has released the funds."

"So I see."

"If you will sign the receipt ..."

"Certainly."

After I had signed, we faced each other again across the desk.

"King's College's Chief Archivist has checked the records," said Ms. Cohen. "A clergyman, the Reverend Cadwallader Simpson, presented the manuscript in question as a gift to the College ..." She glanced at the document on her desk. "The date was November 7, 1862. By the early 1900's, King's College had lost track of the manuscript. Now that the administration has been officially reminded of its existence, the college is delighted and grateful to have it returned."

"Has it been returned already?"

"Yes. The Court released it promptly upon my application. I stressed that the material was fragile. If the Crown wanted to introduce it as evidence, they'd better ensure that it received proper care in the interval."

"It's been around for four hundred years," I pointed out. "It wasn't going to disintegrate in six months."

"Possibly I exaggerated. At any rate, the head of the Conservation Department at the King's College Library is ecstatic about the manuscript. We talked about it on the phone. He's never before had an opportunity to work on a document that old." She turned around a sheet of paper lying on her desk so that I could read it. "He faxed me an outline of the proposed treatment."

I glanced over the list.

Fumigation came first, in order to destroy insects, worms, mould, mildew, fungus, and every imaginable form of microscopic life. Following fumigation, the conservator would encapsulate the individual pages in sheets of Mylar plastic to keep the ancient paper from damage and dirt. After that, the manuscript would be kept at the ideal temperature of 19° to 20° C (66° to 68° F) with humidity maintained below 45 RH.

"Sounds good," I said. "King's College intends to take better care of the manuscript this time."

Feeling somewhat giddy, I wrote Ms. Cohen a cheque to cover her fee.

"Don't try to cash this until I've had time to deposit the funds in my bank account," I warned her while stuffing the packets of money into my briefcase.

We shook hands. "Glad to have been of help," she said.

After leaving the law office, I drove straight to the bank, and from there to Tim Hortons to pick up a chicken salad sandwich and a cruller for my lunch. I should stop eating like this, I told myself as I waited for my order. It was time I learned to cook. That would impress my Mom.

Driving back to Inchbury Street, I noticed that the leaves of the maples that lined the streets were tipped with crimson and gold.

Socrates was waiting on the front porch. He rushed ahead of me into the house when I opened the door, almost tripping me as I stooped to pick up the clutter of envelopes that had fallen through the letter slot. Following Socrates into the kitchen, I dropped the mail onto the table.

I put on the kettle, and then sat down at the table to eat my lunch. Facing me were the letters, bills and brochures that I had picked up. The one on top was a business envelope with no identification. Just an address: 38 Isabella Street, Toronto.

I took a bite of my sandwich. 38 Isabella. Now, where was that?

Then I remembered. It seemed such a long time ago that I had been there.

I did not rush. The kettle was boiling. I went to the cupboard and took my old "English Majors are Novel Lovers" mug from the shelf and dropped an Earl Grey teabag into it. "Here's to you, Guy Gordon," I murmured as I poured boiling water into the mug, "wherever you are."

Having no letter opener handy, I took a paring knife from a drawer, inserted the tip of the blade, and carefully sliced open the envelope. When I pulled out the contents, a smaller, pale blue envelope slipped out from the folds of a business letter. It was a dainty blue envelope. Fancy stationery. The kind only a woman would choose – a woman who liked pretty things. On the front was neatly written, "To My Birth Mother."

My heart was beating fast, but still I did not rush. I laid the blue envelope on the table. *Better read the cover letter first. That's the logical order.* I finished eating my sandwich, wiped my fingers on the paper serviette, and then unfolded the covering letter.

"Toronto Catholic Children's Aid Society," the letterhead stated. I read quickly. Adoption Services wished to inform me that a match had been found. Enclosed was a letter from my daughter. I might answer it if I chose to do so. If I did, I should tell my birth relative something about myself. The letter suggested appropriate subjects: physical description, education, employment, lifestyle, family, and finally motivation for seeking a reunion. But I must give no identifying information: not my name, my address, or even the city where I lived. The letter was signed by Mary Flemming, the social worker who had spoken with me.

I remembered Mary Flemming, her soft grey eyes and cool, level gaze. I remembered just as clearly her cautionary tone when she had asked whether it was a reunion I needed, or simply information. "It's not fair," she had said, "to walk into someone's life, turn it upside down, and then walk out again."

A feeling of fear nudged my heart. I sat there staring at the blue envelope as apprehensively as if I expected a letter bomb to blow up in my face.

I ate my cruller, drank my tea, and studied the neat handwriting that I had never seen before. Then I opened the small, blue envelope.

It held a snapshot of a young couple, and a two-page letter. After a quick glance at the photograph, I read the letter:

> Dear Birth Mother,
>
> I always wanted to know you but my Mom and Dad would of been upset.
>
> So I didn't put in my name in the Adoption Disclosure Register when I could of when I turned 18. But now I'm married and expecting. My baby will be a boy I know this because of having a ultrasound. Just imagine!!!! I want you to share my happiness. In three months you will be a Grandma!!!

I stopped reading. A grandma! Me!

I returned to the letter:

> I dropped out of school in Grade 9 but I want to go back some day and finish.
>
> I am married like I already told you and I am friendly but sort of shy. My husband Jack knows I am looking for you. But my parents dont. Like I said.
>
> I want to meet my half brother's and sister's if you have other kids.
>
> I look forward to learning all about you.
>
> Love,
>
> Your Birth Daughter

Leaning back in my chair, I could hardly catch my breath. "Well," I gasped. "Well, well!" I wanted to know how my daughter had turned out, and now I knew.

I looked at the snapshot. In the background was a baseball diamond, with a small bleacher off to one side. In the foreground, a smiling young couple, both wearing jeans and T-shirts, stood squinting into sunshine, each with an arm around the other's waist. They were the same height. The boy was stocky in build, with a broad, pleasant face and dark blond hair slanting across his forehead. The girl, my daughter, was exceptionally pretty. Apart from the black hair, she looked like me – at least the way I had looked at twenty-one. The hair was from Guy, her father. He did not know that she existed.

Looking at the picture, I couldn't help thinking about Guy. He didn't have much education either. But he was sweet, and considerate, and fun to be with. First love. Had I ever really loved anyone since?

The clock ticked in the front hall. *Tempus Fugit.*

Had I left it too late? Or was this too soon?

Tears filled my eyes, spilled over, and dripped upon the paper as I reread the letter. I knew that I would keep it, along with the snapshot. But I did not know what I could say in my answer. How could I integrate this stranger, her husband, and their child into my life?

On the morning of my meeting with Dr. McBroom, I fed Socrates twice by mistake, scorched my Holt Renfrew suit while pressing it, and ran a red light on my way to the university.

Fortunately, I still had the faculty-parking sticker on my front windshield. By a stroke of luck, I found a parking space right behind Cameron Hall. Walking around to the front entrance, I noticed an empty beer bottle in the shrubbery, lying under the branching boughs of a low juniper. I picked up the bottle and put it in a trashcan.

Pulling open the heavy oak door, I turned down the corridor leading to the Dean of Studies' office. Despite a little quaking at the knees, I was calm as I entered, and with a smile, informed the secretary of my appointment.

No delay this time. Within seconds, she notified the Dean, and the door to the *sanctum sanctorum* opened.

"How do you do, Dr. Gunn?" The Dean's smile stretched his thin lips but failed to reach his eyes. He extended his right hand for me to shake, which I did, and offered me coffee, which I declined. With a brisk gesture, he invited me to sit down on the straight-backed chair that faced his desk. He took his seat in the over-sized leather chair behind it.

On the desk was a document, printed on legal-size paper, to which he turned his attention as soon as we both were sitting. Running his forefinger down the margin, he stopped at one paragraph, and then another. Each time his finger stopped, he uttered a pronounced “humph.”

I shifted in my chair, waiting. Obviously, the document had something to do with me. But Dr. McBroom did not look up as he went on to read the second page, and then the third, which was the last. Below the main signature, there were lines where witnesses had signed their names. Beside the signatures, a big red seal was affixed.

From the wall behind the Dean’s desk, the first Principal of Melrose University, Douglas Mackenzie, D.D., bearded like a patriarch, frowned his disapproval, dark eyes stern under beetling brows.

Upon reaching the end of the document, the Dean raised his head and regarded me along the length of his nose.

“Before leaving Canada, your friend Sir Sebastian Pomeroy paid a visit to the Principal. I gather that he spoke most eloquently about the need to promote the humanities at Melrose University, and to that end proposed the establishment of a Chair in Shakespeare Studies.”

“He did?”

The Dean’s eyes returned to the document. “A most munificent endowment. There has been nothing to equal it this century.”

He must have meant the previous century, since the current one was still in its first decade.

He continued, "Melrose University depends heavily on its endowments."

"Yes. You mentioned that once before."

His face reddened. He looked about to choke.

"This endowment comes with no strings attached."

"Of course not."

"Unlike some institutions of higher learning, Melrose has never permitted benefactors to interfere in matters of faculty appointments, although their suggestions are frequently taken into account." His deep sigh suggested that this was not a matter for rejoicing. "Melrose has been a secular institution for close to one hundred years; nevertheless, its values remain Presbyterian."

"You do realize," I said helpfully, "that Melrose Abbey in Scotland, after which this university was named, was Roman Catholic?"

He looked at me along his nose again, probably sniffing for whiffs of incense and other symptoms of Popery.

"In those days, the faithful had no choice."

"Excuse me," I said. "Did you invite me here to discuss the Protestant Reformation?"

He picked up his fat, black fountain pen and rolled it between his fingers, staring at it intently.

"Without wishing to interfere in matters of academic independence, Sir Sebastian expressed a preference that the University should offer the first appointment of the Chair to the instructor who contributed so greatly to his own appreciation of literature."

I opened my mouth. Nothing came out.

The Dean continued. "This would not be a regular appointment. The term is for five years, renewable upon mutual agreement. The stipend is equivalent to the salary of a full professor, but with one-half of a normal teaching load, the assumption being that the holder of the Chair would engage in research during his or her incumbency. I am given to understand that you do have a significant project underway?"

"Yes," was as much as I could say.

## Acknowledgements

I am grateful to the many people who have provided information, inspiration and so much help. Kevin Peter Clarke introduced me to the professional staff at the Toronto Catholic Children's Aid Society, who answered my questions patiently and meticulously about the procedures for helping adopted children and their birth mothers to find one another. Sgt. Sid Millin and P.C. Alan Drennan of the Hamilton Police Department took the time to provide information about search warrants and search procedures. As always, Chris Pannell, who chaired Hamilton's New Writing Workshop for twelve years, was of inestimable help. Thanks also to Linda Helson, Barbara Ledger, Debbie Welland, and Alexandra Gall of the University Women's Club, Hamilton Branch, and to Allan Briesmaster, Janet Myers and Alison Baxter Lean for their positive criticism and suggestions. Thanks also to Janice Jackson for her brilliant artwork and to Kerry J. Schooley, my literary editor at Seraphim Editions, who for the second time has helped bring my work to fruition. I am grateful to George Down for his careful editing. Finally, I would like to thank my publisher, Maureen Whyte, for her ongoing belief and support.